"The ... we ... ou."

A blaze of rage slashed into Tanya's despair. "Oh, lovely!" she declared at her sarcastic best. "Nothing is sacred from her. She knows it all, doesn't she? She knows more about your feelings for me than I do. Because you tell *her*, and you don't tell *me!*"

Tanya had the grim satisfaction of seeing a look of guilt flicker over his face. "I want you, Tanya. I want you very much."

"I know that, Rafe." It was why he'd married her.

"I'd do just about anything to get you back," he said, obviously hating the necessity, but unable to deny the depth of his desire.

"Wanting is not enough, Rafe," Tanya stated with bitter determination. "There has to be understanding."

EMMA DARCY nearly became an actress until her fiancé declared he preferred to attend the theater *with* her. She became a wife and mother. Later, she took up oil painting—unsuccessfully, she remarks. Then she tried architecture, designing the family home in New South Wales. Next came romance writing—"the hardest and most challenging of all the activities," she confesses.

EMMA DARCY

breaking point

Harlequin Books

TORONTO • NEW YORK • LONDON
AMSTERDAM • PARIS • SYDNEY • HAMBURG
STOCKHOLM • ATHENS • TOKYO • MILAN

Harlequin Presents first edition February 1992
ISBN 0-373-11433-8

BREAKING POINT

CHAPTER ONE

TANYA'S GAZE DRIFTED once more to the Dresden clock on her dressing table. Only a minute had passed since she last looked at it, but every passing minute meant she had less and less chance of changing Rafe's mind about tonight's party. Tanya's frustration and resentment moved up another notch.

In the early months of their marriage Rafe would have telephoned to tell her he was running late. Now she was only given that attention and courtesy if he was going to be very late. Or really very very late. An hour or two didn't count anymore. He just took it for granted she would be here waiting for him. After all, she was *his wife!*

Tears pricked at her eyes.

Where had it all gone wrong?

As the plaintive question revolved in her mind, a harsh cynical laugh broke from her throat. It was such a stupid thought! Their relationship had always been wrong. Right from the start. Only she had been too blinded by her love for Rafe to see it. Blind and young and naive. But she wasn't blind anymore, and she wasn't young anymore, not in her heart, and she certainly wasn't naive anymore.

She blinked away the tears and got on with finishing the first coat of nail polish. Bright red. Red for her anger. Red for her bleeding heart. Red for the fire in her belly. Red for the explosion that could very well end their marriage tonight.

Of course, she knew why Rafe had married her instead of just taking what he wanted of her. It had nothing to do with being in love. It was all about possession. Absolute possession.

Her virginity had surprised him. There weren't many twenty-one-year-old virgins around these days. But then most girls weren't brought up by grandmothers who had strict standards and a moral code that was pure nineteenth-century Victorian.

Grandma had gone out of her way to impress on every boyfriend Tanya had ever had that he was accountable to that formidable old lady for Tanya's well-being. Not that it had stopped them from trying, but Tanya had so many built-in inhibitors against "loose loving" that none had got very far with her. On the other hand, maybe none of them had tried too hard. There were not many people in this life who had ever wanted to be accountable to Grandma over anything, let alone something she felt strongly about.

Until Rafe.

Rafe had not been a boy.

And Rafe went after what he wanted with single-minded ruthlessness.

He had wanted Tanya from the first moment he laid eyes on her and she had had no defenses against him. One look and she was his. After he had taken her virginity he had decided to keep her as his. All his. To have and to hold. And no other man was to so much as look at her, except to admire at a distance. A far distance. Rafe was like Grandma in some ways. Both were winners.

He had been so impatient to marry Tanya that it was more than flattering. It was Grandma who had insisted on a two-month engagement so that a "proper" wedding could be arranged for her granddaughter. Tanya realized now that those two months were the only time in their whole relationship when Rafe had talked openly about his work and shared his life with her. Whatever she had asked of him then, he had given her. Until his ring was on her finger and he had her completely in his possession. Legal, moral, physical, emotional, mental possession. Absolute. Bought and paid for.

She'd had no idea how his mind worked in those early days. She had been deliriously happy with him, happy to give up her job without a second thought when he'd asked it of her. After all, as he said, she wouldn't have time for it once they were married.

Rafe had bought a beautiful house for her—a dream house right on the harbor front at Potts Point, one of the most prestigious places in Sydney. Upstairs it had five bedrooms—each with en suite bathroom—and a private sitting room for her to use as she wished. The entertainment rooms downstairs were pure and utter luxury: music room, billiard room, formal lounge and dining rooms, and the more casual living room, which opened out to the pool area.

Rafe had given her carte blanch to do with it as she pleased. He hired an interior decorator, a *woman* interior decorator, to help her find whatever she wanted, and Tanya had had the time of her life turning the house into their home. Only now did she see that project for what it was. It was an indulgence, exactly the same as giving a child an all-day sucker. It gave her an activity to perform, something pleasant to fill in the day and keep her out of trouble.

Yet not for one minute had she doubted Rafe loved her in those first few months of marriage. They hadn't gone out much, and they couldn't very well entertain at home until the decorating was finished. Besides, Rafe had said he wanted her to himself. And Tanya certainly hadn't minded that. Nothing was more exciting and pleasurable than Rafe making love to her.

She hadn't realized then that any business socializing Rafe did away from the marital home was always done with Niki Sandstrom at his side. But Tanya hadn't known about Niki's place in Rafe's life in those wonderful honeymoon months.

She hadn't even realized that he had separated her from his work life until the decorating was finished. She hadn't really noticed his brushing aside her questions about his business because he always wanted to know about *her* day, what *she* had been doing, what she was planning next, and she had bubbled on about every foolish activity until he took her to bed and they became too immersed in each other to think of talking.

He had indulged her every wish as far as the house and most other things were concerned. He took no hand at all in choosing any of the furnishings. "It's your home, Tanya. I want you to have everything you want," he had said.

"But it's your home too, Rafe," she had protested. "I want to please you as well."

He had given her the smile that melted her bones. "You please me. As long as you're here, I don't even see anything else. And if you're happy, I'm happy."

She had taken that as the most beautiful compliment in the world, not knowing what it meant. Tanya had believed it was because he loved her so much. But it wasn't that at all. He was simply letting her create her own surroundings so she would be happy and content with them. Waiting for him. Waiting for him to come home and take his pleasure in his possession.

There were many meanings she hadn't comprehended until more time had passed: such as Rafe's surprise over her love of antiques and the quietly elegant style of furnishings she preferred.

"I thought you would go for something more exotic," he had remarked. Not in a critical way. More in puzzlement.

She had laughed at him. "Didn't you realize I'm an old-fashioned girl?"

"Of course," he quickly agreed, a deep satisfaction gleaming through his smile. "What else?"

After all, she had been an old-fashioned virgin. And it pleased him to think she had old-fashioned morals. It meant he could count on fidelity in his wife...no matter what! But he didn't think of her as old-fashioned. He thought of her in an entirely different fashion.

Tanya swept a derisive glance around the decor she had chosen for their bedroom. It was soft, romantic, elegant, everything she had ever dreamed of for a bedroom. The rich cream of the carpet was repeated in the bed's padded Queen Anne headboard. The quilted silk bedspread was a quiet pattern of soft greens and mauve and pink on a cream background. The padded pelmet above the large picture window and the deeply sashed side curtains were of the same fabric, setting off the massed folds of cream organza in the rest of the window. Pale green silk armchairs graced two corners, and a magnificent mahogany highboy balanced the beautiful wing-mirrored dressing table where Tanya sat on the matching padded stool.

It was a lady's bedroom.

She should have decorated it like a bordello. Purple carpet, black silk sheets, mirrored ceiling, wildly exotic furniture, animal skins. At least that would have reflected what happened here.

Although Rafe still wouldn't have left any trace of himself to show the room was his as well as hers. That was because his personality lived elsewhere. Here he slept and had sex with his wife. Any bedroom at all would fulfill those purposes. All the interest he had shown in her decorating activities had only been a pose. There was only one thing he was interested in with her.

No, she was wrong about that. There were two things. He liked showing her off. On *his* arm. But that was only supplementary. Besides which, it kept her busy shopping for clothes. And out of trouble.

Once the house was completely furnished, the social entertaining had begun with a vengeance. Parties, theatre outings, charity functions, dinners, keeping Tanya busy, saving Rafe the effort of having to make meaningful conversation with her. The only intimacy he wanted with her was in bed. His precious personal assistant supplied all the meaningful companionship he wanted.

Rafe wouldn't listen to a word against that insidious woman. He didn't listen to Tanya at all. The fights had started slowly at first, usually over something trivial. As Tanya's frustration with their relationship mounted, they became more and more serious. Rafe always gave in first. Except when the issue was important. Then he was as cold and unyielding and unbending as the Himalayan mountains. And completely without any understanding of *her* needs. Rafe's solution to everything was a wild tunmble in bed. SEX. It was his solution to every problem with her.

Like last night.

After the telephone call.

Not content with having Rafe at work all day, Niki Sandstrom had started intruding at home as well! Tanya was furious, that cool supercilious voice asking for *her* husband. Tanya had told her whatever she had to tell Rafe could wait until tomorrow, then slammed the receiver down. Another fight, with Rafe angrily dismissing Tanya's fierce resentment of Niki, then making love to her to dismiss it even further. But it hadn't made Tanya forget her grievances. And *that woman* was not going to be at his side tonight. Not if Tanya could help it.

It had taken a long time for her eyes to be opened to what was really going on. They were open now. And the crunch was certainly coming tonight.

If Rafe wasn't prepared to see her side, to show some understanding, concede just once on something important to her, then Tanya had come to the end of the road. The end of Rafe's road anyhow. She had a right to be a person. She had a right to find achievement beyond running a house and stocking a wardrobe. She had a right to children. She had a right to lots of things that Rafe didn't recognize.

She was not going to be a parakeet kept in a gilded cage for Rafe's insatiable pleasure. No more. No more parakeet. No more cage. If Rafe wasn't prepared to share with her, to let her do what she wanted, just as he did everything he wanted, then he was in for the shock of his life.

It had to stop. It had to change. If he kept on refusing to recognize that their marriage was a hollow sham... Tanya shook her head in wretched despair.

She didn't want to leave him.

She loved him. Desperately.

And wanted him. Wanted him so much it was almost a sickness inside her. He had only to look at her...but that wasn't enough anymore! She needed to be more to him than a sex object. Or a plumaged bird he could display.

He wouldn't even let her have a baby. Not yet, he kept saying. Always *not yet!* Tanya was almost certain he meant never. A heavily pregnant Tanya would interfere with the two things he did want from her. This house, which wasn't a home at all, was always going to remain empty. As empty as their marriage.

Why? Why couldn't Rafe love her as she did him?

The powerful thrum of the Aston Martin echoed up from the driveway below the window. Tanya's heart gave an agitated leap. Rafe was home. He was so late! Would he make love to her? And if he did, what would he do then? Shut her out? Keep his distance? Business as usual? ''Now, Tanya, be a good girl and do as

I say. I make the *important* decisions.'' That was what his manner always implied.

She heard the front door open and close but she pretended she didn't hear. It didn't suit her purpose to run downstairs and welcome him home. She loosened the edges of her robe to give a tantalizing glimpse of cleavage, tightened the belt to emphasize her narrow waist and the voluptuous curve of her hips, then opened the bottle of nail polish and started giving her fingernails a second coat of red.

Now, she thought, *I'll give you what you want, Rafe. Then let's see if there's life after sex.*

CHAPTER TWO

TANYA KNEW PRECISELY when Rafe reached the bedroom doorway, although she went on painting her nails, pretending she didn't. It was almost as though he emitted a force field, which instantly enveloped her. She could feel his eyes burning over her with that calculating possessiveness she had come to hate.

But she couldn't stop herself from responding to it. She could feel awareness crawling through every pore in her skin, squeezing at her heart, burrowing through her stomach, generating a rush of moist heat between her thighs. Even now, when she could almost kill him for not seeing what he was doing to her, he could still arouse her like this, just by a look.

Tanya barely controlled the sudden tremble of her hands as she ran the brush over the last nail. A slash of red overran the cuticle. *Too bad!* she thought viciously. If Rafe insisted on having his own way and going to his damned business party, he could put up with less than perfection tonight. She jammed the brush back into the nail-polish bottle, screwed the lid down tight, then lifted her hands, fingers spread wide, wriggling them for quick drying.

"Wearing red tonight?"

The furry sensuality in his voice instantly thickened her awareness of him. She flicked her gaze up to the mirrors of her dressing table, giving his reflected image a wide-eyed look of surprise. He was lounging indolently against the doorjamb, his suit coat and tie dangling from one hand, the inevitable glass of whisky and ice in the other. His relaxing drink... then his relaxing wife...the switch-off mechanisms from his real life that he wouldn't allow her to share.

She smiled as she thought of the dress she had bought for tonight... if he insisted on going to the party. "No. Black," she replied. Black for mourning. Black for despair. "You should have said hello," she added chidingly.

He smiled back, white teeth flashing the wolfish smile that always excited her... the hunter who had sighted his prey and intended to feast on it. "I didn't want to disturb your concentration," he said, but the telltale simmer in his vivid blue eyes told her his appetite had been whetted by watching her.

As she had intended.

As she had planned.

The short silk wrap she wore was not so much a cover-up as a provocative invitation. The only power she had over Rafe was her sexuality, and the thin clinging fabric left him in no doubt. She was naked underneath. Naked and readily available for his touch and desire.

He pushed away from the doorjamb and strolled purposefully towards her, tossing his coat and tie on the bed as he passed it. Tanya's pulse quickened with each step he took. Rafe was a magnificent male animal, all lean taut flesh and muscle exuding a strength that both threatened and attracted like a magnet. From the moment she had met him he had blotted out the image of every other man, stamping himself on her mind and soul as the only one. She loved him. She wanted him. She needed him. But he was killing her soul.

Tanya remained seated on the padded stool in front of the dressing table, watching him in the central mirror as he came closer and closer. He had the dark olive skin and black hair of his Italian mother. It made his eyes more blue, his teeth more white. He was sinfully handsome. There wouldn't be a woman in the world who could look at him without at least a twinge of wanting to know what it might be like to have him as a lover. To feel his touch. To lose herself in those tantalizing blue eyes, which seemed to hold all the male mysteries that a woman most wanted to know.

The rakish arch of his black eyebrows was a challenge alone. The hard cut of his facial bones was another, denying any strain of softness in the man. But his mouth promised a knowledge that made a woman feel glad she was a woman. His mouth promised both sensuality and sensitivity, and in a purely physical sense it didn't lie.

The mind behind that promising mouth was like a safety-deposit vault, each box neatly labeled and locked away until required for use. Tanya was in the box marked wife, with the subheading sex. She didn't have a key to the rest of his mental vault. But the key she did have was going to be used tonight to pry other keys loose from Rafe. Or blow everything apart.

He curled a hand around her shoulder, his fingers lightly kneading the soft flesh underneath the silk as he leaned over her other shoulder to place his whisky glass on the dressing table. She could see his mind already ticking over, calculating the possibilities, the time . . .

"Mmm . . . new perfume," he murmured approvingly. "Lovely."

"*Poison* by Dior."

"It doesn't smell like poison to me."

She smiled. "We'll see."

He missed the irony. Underneath the exotic aroma the perfume smelled of sex. That was what Rafe liked. Sex. Exotic sex. Exotic Tanya.

She knew that was how he thought of her now, and seeing them both in the mirror, his head above hers, the contrast in their coloring did have a certain fascination that even she had to acknowledge. Her skin was pale and creamy. The deep auburn glow of her hair sprang away from her face in a thick cloud of waves and curls that spilled down to her shoulder blades. Her face was not one of classical beauty but she knew from experience that it held a fascination for men.

Her dark eyebrows rose to a short late curve. Her large eyes were green with a glittering rim of golden specks. Thickly lashed and deeply lidded, they tended to give her a sultry look. Her nose had a pert and very feminine tilt. Her mouth was generous and full lipped. The dimple that broke the smooth oval line of her chin seemed to echo the deep indentation of her upper lip, creating some mysterious effect men seemed to find intriguing.

Rafe's hand dropped away from his glass and swept her hair aside. He bent to kiss her long throat, his lips trailing slowly to her ear as he breathed in the heavy scent. "Salute," he murmured softly. Then predictably, "It suits you."

He slid his tongue around the sensitive whorls of her ear. Tanya half jerked her head away. Not in rejection. Simply from the electric jolt of his eroticism. Rafe's low sexy chuckle told her that he knew that. He knew exactly how she responded to every touch. He reveled in her sensitivity and his power to drive her crazy with desire.

But in this arena at least, it was a two-way thing.

She had to tempt him now. Excite him. Push him past his calculations on time and other things. Then maybe he could be persuaded into staying home with her. All night. And perhaps he would feel indulgent enough to talk to her, to listen to her and to try and understand what she felt. Tanya leaned back, deliberately rubbing against his thighs like a cat acknowledging its owner and wanting to be stroked.

She felt him stiffen. Her eyes flirted with his in the mirror, knowingly, invitingly. His mouth curved in sensual appreciation and the simmer of desire leaped to a bright burning intensity. He pulled her harder against him as his hands slid forward, pushing aside the loose edges of her robe, baring the lush fullness of her breasts.

That's the first step! Tanya thought exultantly. He had thrown aside the time factor. But then Rafe liked living dangerously, right on the knife's edge. He would be planning on quick satisfaction now, but Tanya wasn't about to allow him that.

His tanned brown hands curled slowly around the swell of her breasts, his dark fingers indulgently stroking the white satin smoothness of her flesh while he watched, while they both watched, the stark visual image in the mirror as her nipples tightened into hard prominent buds.

She sensed his deep pleasure at being able to arouse her so easily, so visibly. There was no hiding it. But somehow she had to control it tonight. Make him wait. Make him stay. Make him listen.

Rafe moved his thumbs over the aroused tips in an erotic fan dance, lightly teasing at first, but gradually quickening to a firmer sweep that became unbearably exciting.

Tanya knew he wanted her to break. He was watching so intently, waiting to see. That excited him more than anything else, to see her go wild, to have her mindless with wanting him. Mindless...mindless...mindless. He had Niki to talk to, Niki to share his mind with; Niki, his precious personal assistant who was so indispensable to him. He didn't need a mind in his *wife!* Only a body that satisfied his sexual needs! And Tanya wasn't by any means certain that he didn't share that with Niki, too!

She held on, denying him his triumph as long as she could. The excitement of challenge glittered into his eyes. The tempo of his stroking subsided. He moved his hands in languorously teasing caresses, down to her waist, up under her arms, circling her breasts, deliberately leaving her in trembling uncertainty as to when he would strike at those sensitive points again. She saw his eyes flame with the heat of anticipation as he finally ran his fingers over her nipples in swift rotation.

Tension screamed through her nerves. She could feel the blood pounding in her temples. A hot ache dragged at her thighs and grew more and more insistent. Her green and gold eyes glittered a wildly primitive defiance at him. The need to possess him as deeply as he possessed her surged through her like a turbulent tidal wave. She reached back and dragged her fingernails down his tautly muscled thighs. The leap in the pulsing tension of his body sent a fierce thrill of elation through her.

She saw his eyes dilate. "Cat!" he rasped, his breath hissing between his teeth. His hands dropped to her rib cage. He hauled her off the stool, kicking it carelessly aside as he swung her body around and clamped it to his, making her feel the urgent momentum of his desire with each step that took them to the bed.

She curled her arms tightly around his neck and fastened her mouth to his, kissing him with violent passion, not letting him go even when he laid her on the bed and knelt over her. It was he who wrenched his mouth from hers, rearing back to unfasten his trousers.

"No!" she cried in pained protest. "Not like that, Rafe!"

"Tanya..." The need on his face was explicit. His voice a rasp. He drew in a deep breath, trying to regain control. "You did this deliberately."

"Yes," she admitted.

"Then you know it has to be quick. There's no time for anything else."

"That's nothing more than lust, Rafe," she accused fiercely. "And I'm not in the mood for that."

She rolled over on her side, away from him, attempting to get up. He caught her, pinned her down, his eyes blazing with frustrated desire. "Tanya, you want it. I want it..."

"Not with you fully dressed, Rafe."

"But you do want to make love," he pressed.

Make love, she thought derisively. What a hideous abuse of the English language! Or were love and sex so hopelessly intermingled there was no distinction?

"Yes," she conceded.

His face relaxed into a satisfied smile as he released her and straightened up. "Come and undress me then," he urged, his eyes glinting wickedly.

Rebellion stirred. She wasn't going to let him triumph that easily. She rolled over to the other side of the king-size bed and sat up against the pillows, curling her legs under her. She looked back at him in fiery challenge. "If you want me, you can undress yourself! I'm not your slave, Rafe!"

He laughed mockingly, his hot blue eyes raking over her body as he began unbuttoning his shirt. "Very provocative, my love," he softly taunted.

"Am I your love, Rafe?" she asked hopefully.

He tossed aside his shirt. "You will most certainly be in about ten seconds," he promised . . . or was it threatened?

He means I'll be his possession, Tanya thought miserably, but as she watched the emergence of his sleek virile nakedness, she couldn't stop quivering inside from the strength of her own arousal. He walked around the bed, stalking her, supremely confident in his manhood and its effect on her. Tanya's heart was hammering wildly, but she held his eyes in provocative counterchallenge until he was within reaching distance, then flung herself away from him.

"You'll have to catch me first, Rafe," she tossed at him in defiance.

She wasn't fast enough.

He caught her ankles, hauling her back to him, laughing as he wedged a knee between her legs. He caught her flailing arms and pinned them above her head. His eyes danced exultantly into hers as he lowered his head and took possession of her mouth, invading swiftly, hotly, feeding his passion with hers.

I'll make him forget his damned business, Tanya thought fiercely. *I'll make him forget everything but me.* She fought her mouth away from his. "Let me touch you, Rafe," she whispered huskily.

She would do more than touch him. She would drive him to the limits of his control and beyond. And after it was all over, he would take her in his arms and cuddle her and hug her and tell her he loved her, and there was no one else for him and never would be, because there was no one else like her and she was so unique, so special to him....

"Tanya..."

Her name was a hungry moan that fired her purpose to a new intensity. Rafe was hers! And Niki Sandstrom wasn't going to get any part of him. Not tonight!

He released her arms, his hands finding other targets. His mouth homed onto her breasts. Tanya's fingers streaked into the thick silken blackness of his hair, clutching him to her as he sucked on the throbbing tips, loving the sharp pleasure-pain that speared through her, yet realizing he was already driving her to the edge of climax. *Too fast,* she thought. *Far too fast. Why don't I have any control with this man?*

"Rafe... my wrap," she gasped.

He peeled the silk from her arms with almost rough urgency. His hands moved restlessly, impatiently, possessively over the voluptuous curves of her body as she tossed the garment aside.

She felt frightened, panicky, at what she was about to do. It was a terrible exposure of her need for him, her love for him. *I shouldn't be doing this,* she thought. Yet the answer was that she must. He moved to take her, but she took him in her hands, stopping him. "Not yet," she whispered. "Not yet."

And she levered him onto his back and moved her mouth over his body, giving him the sweet torment of prolonged enthrallment in pleasure-pain, teasing, tasting, caressing. He ran his fingers through her hair, tenderly, entrancingly as he lay still beneath her, unnaturally still for Rafe, as though he were mesmerized by her wanton lack of inhibitions. Little tremors rippled under his skin, flinches of ultrasensitivity. Then suddenly a groan of unbearable need ripped from his throat and Tanya knew there was no more stopping him.

He became the irresistible force, and nothing, not even an earthquake or a tornado could take his mind off his objective now. Yet he took her as he always did, so *knowingly.* Rafe was a master of touch. His penetration was forceful, instant ease for the aching need inside her, then a slow gentle withdrawal for delicious sensations to spread from the contraction. So masterful and masterly, Tanya thought, as he began the heavy pulsing stroking that melted her limbs and sent her mind into limbo. She hoped Niki Sandstrom envied her this. From the bottom of her heart she hoped that.

Somehow she found the strength to wrap her legs around him, holding him, entrapping him, binding him to her. Even as her body ebbed and flowed around each powerful thrust of his, she exulted in his need for her, exulted in the tension that racked his flesh, exulted in the groaned release that drew him deeply into her keeping.

He fell into her arms then, his face buried against her throat, and she cradled him there as he heaved for breath and gradually grew still. She gently stroked his hair, his back, loving him, fiercely wishing this feeling of intense intimacy could cross over into the rest of their marriage. Into the rest of their lives. She wondered why Rafe was so opposed to having children. She didn't understand that aspect of him at all. It seemed to go against all nature. His seed was in her now, seed that could have made their child, if only he would want it as she did.

He stirred, levered himself up to look down at her face. There was an odd questioning look in the blue eyes, an uncertainty that he quickly hooded as he bent to brush his lips over hers.

Now he would take her in his arms, she thought. He would hug her and cuddle her and ask her things and she would answer them. Tanya flicked out her tongue in teasing invitation, wanting him to kiss her with tenderness, with deep deep love. He seemed to hesitate, then pulled away from her, frowning as he glanced at his watch.

No...dear God! No, no no, she pleaded desperately. He can't. He mustn't. How can he?

"We'll be late," he said brusquely.

"Rafe..." She coiled her arms around his neck and pulled him back to her. "Let's not go," she begged.

"Let's stay here." She lowered her lashes, looking at him with sultry promise. "Together."

He was tempted.

"You know we have an appointment, Tanya," he reminded her. "We're already late. We have to go. You know this is important to me."

"More important than us, Rafe?"

He looked at her intently, considering his reply. "That question doesn't deserve an answer, Tanya. You know it's *us* I'm considering."

She moved her body against his in sensual provocation. She pouted her lips. She trailed a hand towards his ear. Anything to keep him with her. "I want you to stay here with me," she said huskily.

He sucked in a quick breath and released a shuddering sigh. His mouth twisted into a rueful smile. "No, Tanya. Enough for now. Save your houri tactics until later, my darling. Then I'll be man enough to meet them," he said, and dropped a light kiss on her lips.

It was an excuse. Rafe was man enough for as much repetitive lovemaking as he wanted. But he'd had his sexual fix. Now it was back to business.

"I can't change your mind?" she asked wistfully. She wanted to be hugged and cuddled, not taken to a business meeting in the disguised form of a party.

"Tanya, I won't put other people out to indulge *our* whims." He meant *her* whims. "Apart from anything else, Niki Sandstrom will be there waiting for me, and we've just finished preparing our strategy for tonight."

He was off the bed and heading for the bathroom before Tanya could do anything else to stop him. Niki!

she thought viciously. Of course he couldn't let his precious paragon down!

"Rafe!" she called, her voice harsh with disappointment and desperation.

He shot a frown at her, halting impatiently for her to tell him what she wanted.

"I don't want to go," she said flatly, knowing he had already switched off, knowing she had lost him, but telling him what she felt anyway.

"Why not?"

Because it's business. Because that bitchy ice-woman will be there and she will look at me with that air of superior condescension that shrivels me up inside. And you will share your thoughts with her, not me. And she loves that. She just loves that, Rafe. She loves sharing the life with you that you won't share with me.

"If you were to suddenly get sick, your personal superwoman could handle everything by herself." She advanced the argument, trying to keep the jealous snipe out of her voice, but not succeeding.

"Niki knows I'm not sick, Tanya," he answered levelly. "And she also knows I'm not about to get sick. Now be a good girl and get dressed. We're running late as it is."

He started to turn away.

"I don't feel like being 'a good girl'!" she burst out resentfully, furious with him for treating her like a child.

He was always doing that, making her feel so much less than the invaluable Niki who was given equal-adult status with him, making her so bitterly conscious of the years that the supertalented blonde had spent at his side, years when Tanya had been a child, more or less. She was only twenty-three to his thirty-four now, but she wasn't a child anymore. He had made her a woman, hadn't he? And she wasn't stupid. She could learn what Niki knew about him if only he would give her the chance.

His lips thinned with vexation at her petulance.

"I feel like being me," she threw at him.

"You are you," he said coldly.

This is the end, Tanya thought. Always sex with Rafe. Nothing else. And the end of sex was the end of everything. "What do you feel when you make love to me, Rafe?" she demanded to know. "What does it feel like to be you?"

"I can't remember," he lied, completely dismissing what he had just had with her.

She stared bleakly at his cold, closed-up face. *Why do I love him?* she thought. *It's so stupid. All he is is a good lover. After that, nothing. No sharing. No revealing. He won't even tell me what he feels when we make love together. Sex,* she reminded herself savagely. *He won't even tell me what he feels when we have sex together.*

"I'm expected at the party Tanya. I'm going to the party. I would like to have my wife at my side. But please yourself. If you don't go, I'll go alone. Is that what you want?"

No! I want you, you impossibly selfish man, she thought furiously. But he had spoken in that ultrareasonable tone that said he was being very patient with her and he was the one in authority. She either stepped into line or took the consequences. Which meant total switch-off.

"Fine!" she snapped. "You go and have your shower, Rafe. Wash all of me off you. And I'll get ready to stand at your side like a good little girl."

He heaved an exasperated sigh. "You are acting like a spoiled brat, Tanya. I think sometimes I've been too patient with you. Indulged your whims too much. I'm starting to lose my patience."

So am I, my dearly beloved husband. So am I, Tanya told him silently. *Let the conflagration begin! Our marriage has just hit crisis point!*

She smiled. "Oh, I promise you I won't act like a spoiled brat tonight, Rafe," she said silkily. "I'll be everything you want me to be."

He gave her a long searching look that she met with limpid innocence. "Fine!" he finally said.

Her low bitter laugh made him glance sharply back at her as he reached the bathroom door. "Go on," she urged. "What are you waiting for? We're running late, remember?"

The door shut after him with an ill-tempered bang.

Tanya laughed again.

It was the laughter of a madwoman about to be burned at the stake for being a witch. But before she burned, Tanya was going to be a very exotic witch!

CHAPTER THREE

RAFE GAVE both shower taps a savage twist and stepped under the hissing spray, not bothering to wait until the water warmed up. He welcomed the cold sting on his skin. He needed it. If he didn't cool down he would explode.

Bitch!

How did he feel?

Wasn't it obvious? He felt as though she had just punched him in the gut! The way she had made love to him, it had turned him inside out, the greatest experience of his life. The look on her face—her beautiful, vividly passionate face—he had thought....

But that didn't mean you could forget everything else and abrogate your responsibilities.

His stomach muscles clenched. He closed his eyes tight and turned his face up to the beat of the water. She had done it to manipulate him. To flex her power over him. To twist him around her finger. Knowingly, deliberately and cold-bloodedly.

Well, he wasn't going to let her get away with it. No way in hell! After almost two years of marriage, he still couldn't look at her without that slow burning urge in his loins. Just thinking of her...but at least he had trained himself to shut that out. He'd never get any business done at all if he kept Tanya in his mind all the time.

He thought of his father, always giving in to his wife. Baby after baby after baby—nine of them—existing on barely subsistence living. And then he died, leaving them to struggle on by themselves. No provision made for the future. Blindly indulgent. Totally irresponsible. Feckless. Hopeless.

But Rafe had fixed that. And what he had accomplished since then . . . it was a rare achievement. And all for the sake of family. Not even Tanya, with all her wiles, would interfere with that. It was sacrosanct.

Why did Tanya want to interfere? He had already shown the world what he could do. He and Niki. He wasn't going to let Tanya drive a wedge in there. He didn't know how he was going to stop it, but somehow he'd damned well rise above it!

He grabbed the soap. Wash her off him! Sometimes he wished he could. But she was in his blood. Like a fever that never went away. He had to learn to control it. It had to stop.

Except he didn't want it to stop.

Well, he had to do something about it, or it would spoil everything.

What more does she want?

He'd given her everything.

He turned the taps off, snatched a towel from the rack and gave himself a brisk rubdown. Time for a change, he thought grimly, and without satisfaction.

Little cat! She had her claws out for Niki, but he wasn't having any of that, either. Tanya was not going to run his life. And it was well past the time she grew up. She had to realize that she had to consider him, at least sometimes.

He shaved his face in growing irritation.

What was her purpose? To own him, lock, stock and barrel? No one could do that to Rafe Carlton. Quite a few had tried but no one had ever done it, and no one was ever going to do it. Not even Tanya. He was his own man. And he would stay in control of his life until the day he died.

Tanya was in a mood.

And he didn't like it one bit.

It was time to teach her a lesson, he thought even more grimly. After all, considering everything he'd given her, what more could she want?

TANYA WAS ONLY just finishing her makeup when Rafe returned to the bedroom, the tangy fresh scent of his after-shave lotion wafting in with him. He had washed her off very thoroughly. There was no smell of sex on him. He was all reprimed for the pristine cut and thrust of business. With his other woman! Or maybe it wasn't so clean. Maybe it wasn't clean at all. Maybe Rafe just dressed it up that way.

He didn't so much as glance at Tanya.

Good old Rafe, she thought cynically. She could read him like a book. He had made up his mind. There would be no changing it. Business—and Niki—always came first.

Now he could take the consequences of that decision!

She followed him over to the wall of built-in wardrobes. He pulled on the black trousers of his formal dinner suit and was doing up the studs of his dress

shirt when she took the black dress from its hanger
and started to step into it, still as naked as he had left
her on the bed.

The action arrested the movement of his hands. He
stood completely still and watched her as she pulled
the dress up, fitted her arms through the strapped
slots, fastened the high-collared band around her
neck, then reached into the deeply slashed cleavage to
position her breasts so that they filled out the soft
black crepe to maximum impact. Apart from the
crossed straps at the back which held the bodice in
place, the dress was cut almost to the swell of her buttocks. She threw Rafe a mocking look, held out her
arms and slowly twirled around, undulating her hips
for good measure.

Something like an animal growl rumbled from his
throat. For a moment he looked as if he were about to
change his mind, tear the dress off her and have his
way with her again. Tanya held her breath expec-
tantly. But he didn't follow through. His mouth
thinned in determination. He picked up a pair of cuff
links and began fitting them through their slots with
sharp angry briskness.

Business!

Definitely business!

She supposed that was where he got his charge
from. It fed his ego. Together with a pretty wife he
could display to advantage. To Rafe, that was the
whole of life. He wanted nothing more. Not even
children.

But since *display* was the name of the game, he was
going to get it tonight! Tanya lifted her hands and
ruffled her hair, making sure every voluptuous curve

of her body was being flaunted at him. "Do you like my dress, Rafe?" she asked silkily.

"No."

That hurt. "What's wrong with it?" she demanded.

"Do you enjoy making a public exhibition of yourself?" he bit out.

"Isn't that what you want?" she taunted.

"You'll have the eyes of every man there glued on you," he replied angrily.

"Then that should make you feel good," she retorted bitterly. "Knowing you're the one in possession."

A dangerous glitter made his blue eyes even more vivid. "Stop fooling around, Tanya. What happens in our bedroom is private."

"I don't feel like locking it away, Rafe," she mocked.

"Oh, for God's sake! Be reasonable!" he snapped impatiently. "In that dress you might as well be naked! For all the world you look as though you've just been ravished...."

"Well, I have, haven't I?"

"...and you're wanting to be ravished again."

"I do. Again and again, Rafe."

She boldly ran her eyes down his body with all the hot possessiveness that was seething through her blood. *You're mine, Rafe Carlton,* she thought fiercely. *And Niki Sandstrom is going to know you're mine! Because you won't be able to keep your eyes off me tonight. You won't dare. Because all those other men will have their eyes glued to me. And that's go-*

*ing to make you insecure about your absolute posses-
sion!*

She heard Rafe's breath rush from his lungs in an
unsteady hiss as her eyes smoldered down the fly of his
trousers. Saw the quick rise and fall of his chest as he
took in more air, fast shallow sips of it. Saw his hands
clench. Felt the tension screaming from him as he
fought for control. His all-important shut-her-out
control! Her eyes lifted to his, her lashes half-lowered
in a searing sultry invitation.

It seemed to inflame him. Accelerate his anger. A
slash of red jagged across his cheekbones. His eyes
blazed with the ferocity of a wild animal that was cor-
nered but would never give up. Never! He would fight
to the death.

Through clenched teeth he commanded, "Change
out of that dress!"

Tanya raised her eyebrows in mocking disdain of his
anger. She turned and pretended to examine the line
of dresses in her wardrobe, then bent to the shoe rack,
picked up her strappy black high heels and sauntered
over to the bed, swinging her hips, aware of the
movement of her buttocks sliding against the soft
black crepe that lightly skimmed them and hugged her
thighs.

"Are you ever unfaithful, Rafe?" she asked without glancing back at him. She knew where his gaze was
fastened. She could feel it burning through the thin
layer of black. Black for sex. Black for the anger in her
heart. Black for the death of their marriage.

"Tanya…" There was an ominous threat in the low
growl.

She shrugged and sat down. "We'll definitely be late if you don't hurry and finish dressing, Rafe," she remarked, sliding him a mocking look from under her lashes as she bent to slip the shoes onto her feet.

He muttered something savage under his breath, stepped over to her section of the wardrobe, hauled out a green silk dress and hurled it onto the bed beside her.

"Wear that!" he demanded. "And at least look respectable!"

She looked at the green gown, then lifted fiercely challenging eyes to his. "I'm not in the mood for the ornament-on-the-arm role, Rafe. Not tonight. And I won't ever be again."

The red on his cheekbones was hotter. "Stay at home then!" he snapped.

"With you?" she shot back at him. Without hope.

"No! I'm going!" he grated, his hands making a mess of his bow tie in his anger.

She stood up, walked back to the wardrobe, removed her black beaded evening bag, then walked purposefully over to the dressing table to collect her lipstick and compact. She knew his eyes were glued to her all the way and she made every step a blatant provocation.

"If you're going, I'm going," she said decisively, dropping the makeup she needed into the bag. "There's no two ways about it."

"Not in that dress!" he seethed.

She turned and faced him, sheer mutiny on her face. "Yes, I am, Rafe. In this dress. If you don't take me, I'll get there by myself. And I'll make damned sure everyone knows I'm your wife! And as debasing as it

is, they'll all know why you want me as your wife!
They'll be looking at the real reason, won't they, Rafe?
Won't they?''

He looked at her as though she'd gone stark raving
mad. "What the hell does that mean? What's got into
you, Tanya?" he demanded harshly.

She threw her chin up high. "Why, you have, Rafe.
'Getting into me' is what you married me for. I'm your
legal whore. So why pretend anything else? You don't
want me to have a baby. You don't want me to work
with you. You don't want to talk to me about your
business. You don't want to share your thoughts with
me. The only thing you really want with me is sex.''
Tears glittered in her eyes as she added, "And that's
the only part of you that you give me. Or have ever
given me. Everything else is worthless.''

His face went white. Whether from anger or shock,
Tanya couldn't tell. He looked appalled. Perhaps he
was recoiling from the uncharacteristic crudity of the
terms she had flung at him, or from being hit with
facts that he didn't want to face. He made a slicing
gesture with one hand as though he wanted to dismiss
all she'd said, but he lifted the other and rubbed at his
forehead in some agitation of mind. His lips compressed, still full of determination.

"That's not true," he muttered. "That's simply not
true.''

"Isn't it, Rafe?" she tossed at him bitterly.

Blue eyes clashed with green. "I'm not against us
having a family. I told you that. Is waiting a few more
years so unreasonable?''

There was no point in answering. It was his stock
evasion. Tanya knew he didn't want to share her with

a baby. He wanted exclusive rights. Absolute possession. At least until his obsession with her body was sated. Then, maybe, he wouldn't mind her getting pregnant. And when her body was full and swollen and ungainly and unattractive with his seed, he would have someone else at his side.

When she didn't speak, he took that as a point to him and reached into the wardrobe for his dinner jacket. "I don't want to live business twenty-four hours a day," he said irritably. "If I bring it home to you, I never get away from it. We've been through that before, Tanya. I thought you understood it."

"No, I accepted the excuse, Rafe. I never understood it," she answered flatly. "I reluctantly accepted it because you gave me no other choice. But I don't accept being shut out of all the things that are important to you."

"You are the only important thing to me, Tanya," he insisted. "I don't shut you out."

Her green eyes glittered scorn for the lie he had just told. "That's why we're going to this rotten business meeting tonight instead of staying home together," she snapped.

Because she was right it made him even more angry. "That also is for us," he grated unevenly. "Although your vision is so limited, you don't see it."

Thanks for the put-down, Rafe, Tanya thought bitterly. *That's what you always do. Childish Tanya. Narrow Tanya. Poor dim Tanya who doesn't have the brains to recognize anything important. But she's got a good body for what you want to do in bed.*

She forced herself to inject mildness into her voice. "I'm not important enough for you to put me ahead of Niki Sandstrom. Not important enough to have—'' She nearly said children, but he had already dismissed that subject and it was too painful to pursue when he was totally unsympathetic to it. So she simply concluded with ''—to share anything else together.''

"We share *everything* that's important," he said grimly.

That was another lie. Her eyes held his in savage mockery. "Are you saying that your business with your very confidential assistant isn't important to you, Rafe?"

His face twisted into an exasperated grimace. "Not that again!" he muttered in disgust. The blue eyes flashed furious impatience with her. "If I've told you once, I've told you a thousand times, there's nothing between Niki and me but business. There never has been and never will be. I am not going to fire her because of some crazy jealous idea you've got in your head. And I'm fed up with your harping on it. I never want that subject brought up for discussion ever again."

Because he didn't want to acknowledge the truth of it, Tanya thought bleakly. Niki Sandstrom was his real wife in everything but sharing his bed. And losing her would be a far bigger loss to him than losing Tanya. She wasn't crazy. Rafe just didn't want to see the way his *other woman* kept undermining the kind of relationship Tanya desperately wanted to have with him. It suited both of them better not to.

Niki was playing a waiting game, too. Only she was waiting for Rafe to reach burn-out with Tanya. Then she would have him totally to herself. She would be ever so sympathetic, ever so understanding...and that would be the end of Rafe. The Tanya-mistake would have taught him such a chastening lesson he would walk right into her waiting arms and never look elsewhere again.

Rafe slid his arms into his dinner jacket and buttoned it as he walked over to her, rearranging the expression on his face on the way.

Locking the anger away, Tanya thought in grim acknowledgment of his ability to control himself when he wanted to enough. Master of the situation. That was Rafe. Now he would use his reasonable sweet-tempered tone of voice. His face would reflect a relaxed amusement at the absurdity of such a trivial argument.

Rafe just hadn't got the hang of this situation yet. But he would, Tanya silently promised him. She wasn't going to let him get away with what he was doing to her.

His eyes roved over her in wry appreciation. His mouth curved into a relaxed smile. "Let's drop this absurd argument and have a good time together," he suggested reasonably, his tone full of soft appeasement. "You can wear that dress for me any time you wish. Tonight I would prefer not to have other men ogling what is mine."

He brought a finger up and gently stroked the dimple in her chin as he smiled into her eyes. "It's you I love, Tanya. You I married. You I want to be with for the rest of my life. Now please...change into the green dress and let's get on our way."

"I don't mind other women ogling you, Rafe," she stated flatly. Except, of course, Niki Sandstrom, but as Rafe had just forbidden her to mention that subject again, she could hardly return to it. It obviously wouldn't get her anywhere right now.

His eyes hardened before he could stop them. He took a long deep breath, forcing himself to relax again. "Don't you want to please me, Tanya?" he asked appealingly.

Emotional blackmail!

Tanya lifted her chin away from his touch and walked towards the door.

"Tanya!"

She swung around, her eyes savagely mocking. "If I'm yours, Rafe, you don't have to worry about other men. If you love me, you won't care what clothes I wear, because the person I am is more important to you than anything else. And if you want me to spend the rest of my life with you, you'd better start revising the way you want to spend it, because I don't like what we've got."

His face tightened. The red slashes reappeared on his cheekbones. The blue eyes were as bright and sharp as lasers as they tried to probe her thoughts. "You've never said that before," he accused.

"I thought I'd said it a thousand times in a thousand different ways. You just don't listen to what you don't want to hear, Rafe. Perhaps it needed to be said more directly. More bluntly. I'm glad you heard it this time."

He shook his head. "Why are you doing this, Tanya? Why..."

His voice trailed off as he came to think the unthinkable. His possession had opened the door of her cage, and might, just might, prefer freedom and fly away.

"Believe what you want, Rafe," Tanya cut in acidly, then shrugged as she turned and resumed her walk to the door. "You always do anyway. You're totally selfish in having your own way."

"Tanya!"

She stopped and looked back.

The anger had exploded out of its locked box. The muscles of his face had contracted with the ferocity of his feeling. She could feel electricity crackling from him as he advanced ominously towards her. The fingers of his hands worked furiously and she could see the tension in his arms.

He wants to hit me, she thought in surprise. *If I were a man, he would.* She surprised herself with the thought that she didn't care. In fact, she almost wanted him to hit her. That would finalize everything.

She lifted her face defiantly as he paused in front of her. The challenge sparked brilliantly in her eyes. *Go on. Do it, Rafe. After all, I'm only a possession, not a person. Prove that to me once and for all.*

His chest heaved as he drew in a steadying breath. His eyes blazed murder but he spoke with icy control. "I've given you everything you've ever wanted."

"You've given me what you wanted to give. You've given me nothing that was important to me," she retorted.

A muscle contracted in his cheek. She saw his right hand start to lift. *Now we both know the truth,* Tanya thought grimly, but he fought for control and regained it. His fingers bit into her shoulder. Dug fiercely.

"If that's the way you feel, then go and find what *you* want elsewhere," he grated. "I don't want a rider on my back."

She looked up into his eyes, trying to understand him, understanding him too well. Tears moistened her lashes but she managed to stem their flow. "If that's the way you feel, Rafe, you don't leave me any real choice. I think I'll have to."

His breath was released in a burning hiss. He picked his fingers off her shoulder, stepped back. The blue eyes bored into her with searing intensity for several long moments.

"Tell me when you make up your mind," he said brusquely, then looked at his watch. "In the meantime there are things I have to attend to. I'll say goodbye now. I presume you don't want to be kissed before I go."

Tanya could feel her lips starting to quiver. She bit them. Her heart felt like lead. But she held her head high and her eyes held his in proud bitter defiance. "Oh, I'm still coming with you, Rafe. I'm going to see this night through to the end. The very end."

Then before he could reject her, she added, "One way or another I'll be at that party. You can either take me there or see me there, Rafe. You have a very clear choice. Tell me when you make up your mind."

Pride won.

As she knew it would.

She was still his wife!

For tonight.

But the crunch had come, and where it would end Tanya had no idea. The fire was lit, burning and out of control, and she didn't care if she was consumed by it. But she'd take Rafe through the flames with her before she went. He wouldn't walk away from tonight unscathed.

CHAPTER FOUR

THE SILENCE in the car was thick with tension as they headed into the city. There was nothing to be said by either one. At least she had disturbed him, Tanya thought with grim satisfaction. Rafe was not driving with his usual smooth precision. In fact, the gear box of the Aston Martin was being most uncharacteristically abused. Which meant she had disturbed the smooth planned progression of his life.

I wanted to share with you, Rafe, she mentally pleaded with him. *I wanted your baby. Why was that too much to ask?*

"What do you plan on achieving tonight, Rafe?" she asked tonelessly, hopelessly. "What was worth this?" Even if he bent just a little bit, made some small shift her way, gave her a crumb or two of his real life...

His lips compressed into a thin line. "Dammit, Tanya! What does it really matter?"

It would mean everything to me, she thought, but the savage slice in his voice cut her off from any further approach.

Yet it wasn't true that Rafe was completely selfish. To his family he was generosity personified. In material ways, he gave Tanya everything she wanted. It was himself he wouldn't share.

To some extent she could understand it. With his dirt-poor background, she could see how his driving desire to succeed had been forged. The ambition. The need to own and possess. Rafe had been deprived in every material sense. Yet he belonged to a close and very loving family.

A demonstrative family.

Rafe, alone of all of them, kept what he thought and felt to himself. He never talked about his feelings. He always brushed aside any probing of his emotions and very rarely showed any visible signs of what was going on inside him. Totally unlike his sisters and brothers and his Italian mother, who was the most volubly emotional person Tanya had ever met.

Was that why he was so closed up? Tanya wondered. Was his iron control a reaction against his mother's wildly expressive emotionalism?

Tanya shook her head. Impossible to tell with Rafe. Tanya herself was grateful for Sophia Carlton's openness. Most of what she knew about Rafe had come from his mother. To Sophia, Rafe was little short of being a god.

He was the eldest of her nine children, her first son, her wonderful boy, who had taken care of everything when his father had died, saving them all from poverty when the future had looked impossibly bleak. Only eighteen he had been then, but so smart, too smart for the property dealer who had wanted to buy up their dairy farm for peanuts.

Rafe had worked out that it was their land that was valuable, not the farm. Situated as it was on the outskirts of Sydney, the land could be subdivided into small lots and sold as home sites. Rafe had found a partner for the project and the money he had made for them was the beginning of his personal fortune.

His entrepreneurial enterprises had rapidly built a sizable position in real estate. When it came to buying and selling property, Rafe was the shrewdest dealer in the business. His plans, dreams and daring intrigued his peers. Never a mistake. Always going on to bigger and bigger things.

Sophia never had to worry about money again. Rafe took care of it. And he saw that all his sisters and brothers were well provided for. No mother could have asked for a better son. It was the wife who had problems. Sophia was full of adoration.

Rafe had always been such a wonderful boy, so dependable, so levelheaded, such a tower of strength for his mother, helping to care for the little ones when the family was young, making sure that everything ran right. Anything Sophia had ever asked Rafe to do, he did. He never let her down. Not once. Even that time when his little sister, Maria, was born at home because his father was away and Sophia couldn't get to the hospital. Rafe had taken care of everything. And only thirteen years old then.

In trying to account for Rafe's refusal to let her have a baby—*not yet*—Tanya had wondered if witnessing the birth of his sister had had some traumatic effect on him. But when she'd asked him, the mocking amusement in his eyes had instantly refuted that idea. He had dryly remarked that he'd seen plenty of baby animals born on the farm, and helped in quite a few difficult births. Delivering a child was not much different.

Tanya wondered if he'd had a surfeit of looking after a family, and didn't want more of that kind of responsibility. Yet he showed no resentment of his younger brothers and sisters. He loved each and every one of them. Tanya was certain of that. He always dealt with them kindly and generously. And they all looked up to him as though *he* were their father. He was, without a doubt, their authority figure, and seemed to have been for a long, long time, even before their father's death. It made Tanya wonder what Rafe's father had actually been like.

Sophia spoke of her husband with deep affection and intense loyalty. A wonderful, loving, giving man. More often than not she would have tears in her eyes. Rafe's brothers and sisters remembered their father with love. But Rafe never, never, spoke of him, except in the barest briefest factual terms.

As much as she thought about it, Tanya still had no definite answers as to why Rafe was the way he was. All she knew was that he had no sympathy to her need for a family of her own. He couldn't conceive what it was like to have been an only child. The loneliness. The craving for the closeness of brothers and sisters.

Her parents had died when Tanya was only a baby— a tragic yachting accident when their sailboat was sunk in a sudden squall. Tanya's grandmother had been looking after her on that fatal day, and continued to do so for the rest of Tanya's life. Her grandmother was the only family Tanya had ever had. Not that she could blame Rafe for that. But he could have tried to understand how she felt.

Of course, she loved her grandmother dearly; but she had dreamed of having children—at least two—

when she got married. She desperately wanted to have a baby. She wanted Rafe to want a baby. But he didn't. He just didn't. He pretended to listen to her, pretended to be sympathetic, but always the decision... *not yet!*

He was never going to give in to her.

Never.

He wanted to be the one in control all the time. And he certainly didn't want to share Tanya with someone else, not even their own child!

Tanya couldn't help wondering why he'd married her if he never meant to have children. What was a marriage without children? The answer was all too palpable, and extremely hurtful. She was an object to be owned, for his exclusive use...when the desire and whim to use her overtook him. Mutual possession, he called it. Except she didn't possess Rafe. Niki Sandstrom had more of him than she did.

The fire licked at Tanya's mind.

Rafe had to make his choice tonight. One way or the other, Tanya wasn't going to live with *that woman* anymore. Rafe had to decide which one he wanted to spend his life with, because he wasn't going to have both of them.

Not that Tanya had any idea of replacing Niki in the business. She couldn't. But there was no reason why Rafe couldn't let his wife work as his secretary. Tanya was good at that. Good at research, too. She had already proved that in the job she had held before their marriage. She was not just an object or an ornament. She had a quick mind and a meticulous grasp of detail. The way she had decorated the house should have shown Rafe how thorough and painstaking she could be.

They joined the line of cars waiting to pull into the driveway of the Sheraton Wentworth. Tanya stole a glance at Rafe. His face was stony, totally uncommunicative. She ran the fingernails of one hand along the thick strong muscles of his thigh, just to remind him what they did share. And they could build on that. Their relationship was not doomed, not if Rafe would cooperate even in the smallest way.

His leg jerked away. He picked up her hand, and held it away from him as he turned blazing eyes to hers.

"Don't try any more of those female games on me, Tanya. I assure you, they'll have a far more negative effect than you'd ever bargain for."

"How more negative can you get than total rejection?" she retorted mockingly. "And I wouldn't do that tonight if I were you, Rafe. I'm in the mood for blood and I intend to get it."

Their eyes warred in bitter contest.

A horn honked from the car waiting behind them.

Rafe threw her hand onto her lap, pressed his foot on the accelerator and burned rubber up to the entrance where a doorman stood ready to greet them.

Rafe was definitely disturbed.

Tanya's door was opened for her by a footman. She stepped out of the car at the same time she heard Rafe's door slam behind him. Someone on the pavement behind her wolf-whistled. Several more wolf whistles followed as she moved forward to the red carpet that led into the foyer. She didn't acknowledge them in any way. She waited for Rafe to join her, which he did very briskly.

He didn't link her arm with his as was his usual custom. His arm went around her waist, his hand resting possessively on her hip, holding her close to him as he urged her forward. She wondered if Rafe's arm would be glued across her bare back all night. She didn't mind in the least if it was. With their thighs brushing together like this, Rafe had to be as aware of her as she was of him. He certainly wasn't about to forget her in a hurry. Or shut her out.

Every head in the foyer turned their way as they walked towards the huge chandelier in front of the elevators. Tanya knew they made a striking couple. The women inevitably looked at Rafe first, then at her to appraise the kind of woman he was with. Tonight, none of the men bothered to look at Rafe to see whom she was with. Their eyes kept eating her up. And Tanya hoped Rafe was burning.

He halted after a few meters and half swung her towards him. He looked sternly into her eyes. His voice was a sibilant urgent whisper, full of warning. "From here on in our private problems are put aside, Tanya. Remember that. Whatever your true state of mind, I want you to look the absolute adoring wife. If you don't do that for me, I'll never forgive you. Do you understand?" he finished harshly.

He meant it. There was relentless steel in those blue eyes. If she rebelled against this dictate, it would very definitely be the end. No further chances to change his mind. Finis!

As much as she hated the role he was now thrusting upon her, Tanya dumbly nodded her head. She didn't really want to lose Rafe. It tore her heart out to even contemplate it. She would try...one more act...for him.

His mouth flashed its dazzling smile at her.

Tanya's stomach curled. Even now she wanted him. And the wanting squeezed Tanya's heart with all the misery of loving a man who didn't really care for her. Nevertheless, she dutifully gave him an adoring smile back.

So this is where the acting begins, she thought. *From here on in I'm just for display purposes so Rafe can perform. But he'd better start doing some performing for me as well. And not just in bed!*

They moved on. Rafe halted her again under the huge central chandelier, half turning to scan the bar area to the right of the elevators. Niki Sandstrom instantly rose from an armchair in the closest seating area.

Tall, composed, she had a refined elegance that came close to real beauty—iceberg-cold beauty—and a mind that Rafe admired. Not like his stupid, pretty vacuous wife. Except that wasn't true. Tanya knew she wasn't in Niki's class as a business brain, but she had capabilities enough to be a real help to Rafe. If only he would let her. And then she would be able to share Rafe's thoughts and understand what he was doing.

Niki's shiny white-blonde hair was sleekly groomed into a French pleat. She had chosen to wear an ice-blue dress, which made the most of her slim figure. The cleanly chiseled features of her face tightened for a moment as she took in the wild cloud of Tanya's dark-red hair and the black dress that accentuated every voluptuous curve of Tanya's body. Almost instantly she smoothed her face back to cool serenity.

Diamond earrings sparkled in her lobes.

A gift from Rafe?

As she approached them, Niki glanced pointedly at a diamond-studded watch. The diamonds formed the initial *N*. Definitely from Rafe. He knew how to charm and flatter better than most people. The watch was definitely a gift from Rafe.

Tanya leaned into Rafe's body, making her own explicit claim of possession.

Niki fastened a polite little smile on her lips and met Tanya's fiery green eyes with her cool wintry gray. "Good evening, Tanya," she said with the contemptuous indulgence of an adult to a particularly fractious child who could not be openly reprimanded.

Politeness, of course, demanded something from Tanya. For the rest of the evening she would be ignored, except for the odd condescending smile. Tanya could almost hear her wondering why Rafe wasted his time on his toy wife. While the super-cool blonde could only *guess,* Tanya *knew,* and the reason hurt. The other woman's perception was all too accurate. However, Tanya wasn't about to let Niki Sandstrom rest too comfortably on her laurels with Rafe.

"Good evening, Niki," she drawled huskily. "Sorry we're late. Rafe and I had a few things to settle before leaving home." Since Rafe had asked her to project adoration she would start right here. She slid him a sultry cat-who's-had-the-cream look from under her lashes. "Didn't we, darling?"

"Yes," he answered, granting her a brief indulgent smile before stabbing his gaze back at Niki.

The iceberg bitch sighed in mild exasperation. Her thoughts were clearly revealed. *Men really are the end,* she seemed to say. *Fancy taking the time to do* that *to her when what* is *important is really here.* But, of course, the fact that Rafe did such things only increased the intrigue and mystery that women felt about him. He was a challenge. They wanted to know if they could get him to do such things to them.

Niki reconcentrated her mind on the area where she could always hold Rafe's attention. "They went up twenty minutes ago," she informed him, both of them effectively cutting Tanya out of their mutual understanding. "I turned the situation to our advantage. I told Yorgansson you were receiving alternative offers. You had to consider them."

"Maybe I was," Rafe grated out.

Tanya's heart leaped with wild hope. She looked up at him in swift appeal but his expression was grim, reserved, giving nothing away.

Niki Sandstrom looked thunderstruck. "Whether you did or not," she said uneasily, "I could feel the greed exuding from their pores. We've got them in the palms of our hands," she added with a pointed claim on Rafe's confidence.

"Let's get moving," he replied, immediately drawing Tanya towards the elevators.

Niki fell into step on Rafe's other side. "They came with our competitors," she informed him. "They're trying to frighten you."

"I expected that," Rafe said with a nod.

"Who are your competitors?" Tanya asked.

Niki raised an eyebrow at Rafe, as if to say that was for him to handle if he had to drag his stupid wife along to important business meetings.

Rafe threw Tanya a quelling look.

"I want to know," she said softly, holding his eyes in urgent appeal.

"Keegan and Halsey," he replied, tersely naming a rival real estate company.

Tanya gave him a force-ten adoring smile that kept Rafe's gaze on her face for several seconds. When he finally looked away, Tanya deliberately transferred the smile to Niki. *So take that, you bitch,* she thought venomously. It was the first time Rafe had opened up to her. And in front of her arch-rival.

The gray eyes glittered a weary derision and then dismissed Tanya as of no account.

The elevator doors opened. Rafe waved Niki forward, then swept Tanya in after her, making sure he stood between the two of them in the small compartment. His body was tense. The atmosphere in the elevator was thick with things unspoken as they traveled upwards.

Tanya was not at all happy with the blonde's pointed dismissal of her. It was too confident. Which meant she was very very sure of her place in Rafe's life. Tanya wondered just how much Niki Sandstrom had influenced Rafe in the attitude he had taken towards his child-wife. Oh, she would do it so cleverly, sliding in the odd comment here and there in her sweet-acid patronizing way.

Tanya knew that Niki hated her. Rafe never saw it because the ice-cool blonde was meticulously polite to her in front of him. But the few times they shared a

powder room together, the gray eyes had given Tanya
their unmistakable message. Hatred. Undiluted.

In one way, Tanya didn't blame her. The other
woman had given Rafe ten years of her life, only to see
him marry someone ten years younger than she. A
sexual aberration that would pass in time. That was
what she was counting on. And if Tanya couldn't
make their marriage more than just a sexual aberration, Niki would probably win in the end.

But Tanya was winning very slightly on points tonight. So far.

They alighted at the ballroom floor and were
quickly swept into a crowd of people and innocuous
greetings. The party was ostensibly a fund-raiser for
charity and the guest list was virtually a "Who's
Who" in Sydney. It was the kind of affair that social-
ites attended to show off their latest designer dresses
and their men came along to chat with their peers
about the latest coups in the business world. It was
also the place where informal talks could lead to un-
derstandings, relationships cemented and important
decisions made.

Champagne flowed. Waiters circulated with trays of
hors d'oeuvres. A band played a string of popular hits.
Not too loudly. Rafe put on a genial face but his arm
remained glued around Tanya's waist. Despite his
good-humored mask and manner, he was not at ease.

He was even less at ease when he and Niki finally
homed in on the man they had come to influence. In-
troductions were made. Yorgan Yorgansson was a tall
blonde Dane—around fifty, Tanya judged from the
streaks of silver in his fair hair—and still an impressive figure of a man. Although most men looked im-

pressive in formal dress, Tanya amended. His face was
a little heavy with maturity, but still good-looking. His
blue eyes were lighter than Rafe's and they had that
same laid-back calculating quality. Tanya couldn't
help but notice that because his eyes looked at Tanya
continuously... appreciatively.

Rafe seemed to have a problem concentrating his
mind. His pluperfect assistant tactfully filled in any
gaps in the conversation, which remained general for
much longer than Tanya had anticipated. It circled
around the present turnover in big Sydney properties,
particularly to Japanese investors, but did not get
down to any nitty-gritty discussion of the project they
were really interested in. Niki made a few deft at-
tempts to prompt Rafe into more precision, but he
didn't follow through. And neither did Yorgan Yorgansson.

Finally Rafe turned to Tanya with an indulgent
smile. "Darling, we must be boring you. Why not go
off and enjoy yourself. Niki and I..."

Dismissed from the important arena! Cut out. Shut
off. Well, not tonight, husband dear, Tanya determined. *You want an act? I'll give you an act that will
sizzle your socks!*

She flashed him an adoring look, although it almost killed her. "I'm having the time of my life right
here with you, Rafe darling," she sweetly crooned,
injecting a sexy huskiness into her voice.

"Yes," said Yorgan. "If your wife doesn't find me
too old and boring..."

"Tanya loves to dance," Rafe grated out, his eyes
glinting dangerously, his meaning all too clear to

Tanya. *You're interfering,* it said. *You're a distraction that I don't want right now! Neither want, nor need!*

"Then may I," said Yorgan, "have the pleasure?" He offered his hand in persuasive invitation.

Oh, God! thought Tanya. *This is going all wrong!* She could see the look of suppressed fury on Rafe's face. Numbly she took Yorgan's hand and let him lead her off. What else could she do? To refuse him, after Rafe's declaration that she loved to dance, would be like a slap in the face. Yet she knew it was the last thing Rafe wanted...for her to take Yorgan away from him and Niki.

Rafe can't put the entire blame on me, Tanya thought frantically. But as Yorgan drew her close to him, and his fingers slid sensually down the curve of her spine—her bare-skinned spine—she knew with utter certainty that Rafe would place the entire blame on her. Her defiance of his command to change her dress for something more respectable was the nail in her coffin. *A black coffin,* she thought despairingly.

Why, oh why did the best-laid plans go astray?

Yorgan was an expert dancer but Tanya couldn't lift herself beyond a wooden response. He kept talking to her about Rafe's plans, trying to draw her out, but since Tanya knew nothing about Rafe's plans she could only reply with meaningless platitudes. *Is this why Rafe keeps me ignorant?* she wondered. *So I can't say anything to hurt his plans?* The thought added another depth of sickness to her despair. Couldn't he even trust her a little bit?

When it became obvious to Yorgan that Tanya knew nothing that might help him in his dealings with Rafe, he pursued a different line. A silent tactile line that told Tanya he found her tantalizingly desirable and if she was interested, he most certainly was. He drew her closer so that her thighs brushed his. Nothing too obvious. Nothing offensive. Just an edge of offered intimacy. He was a subtle man, not a crass one. His hand splayed over the pit of Tanya's back, enjoying the curve of her body, fingers testing the smooth satin of her skin.

Tanya died a thousand deaths. She could feel Rafe's eyes like daggers ripping through her. She knew that most of her value to him was in being his absolute possession, and she had deliberately invited this other man to touch her by wearing this dress. That was what Rafe would think. That was what everyone in the ballroom would think. Anyone who wore this kind of dress was asking to be touched. Except Tanya had only wanted Rafe's touch.

Her skin burned with guilty shame and embarrassment. She kept her eyes lowered from Yorgan's, giving him no encouragement whatsoever. She feverishly wondered if she should reach back and yank his hand up. But that would be crass. She didn't want to make a spectacle over something that other lookers-on would see as perfectly normal. And it would probably make Rafe even more furious with her.

The music finally stopped. Yorgan led her back to Rafe. And Niki. The expressions on their faces were clearly readable.

Rafe's was totally closed. There was a blank bored look in his eyes. No flash of adoration from him. Not even a flash of fury. Tanya had let him down in everything he counted as important, and she no longer had any value to him. Not as an ornament, nor as a possession.

Niki's face was composed into one of long-suffering patience. But there was a glint in her eyes that said her reward was just around the corner.

"Thank you for the dance, Mr. Yorgansson," Tanya managed to force out evenly. "If you'll excuse me..." She cast a fixed look of polite retreat around them all, then fled to the powder room.

Tanya had no awareness whatsoever that every eye in the ballroom followed her as she walked towards the foyer. She didn't feel Rafe's gaze burning after her. Her mind was focused inward. The glint of triumph she had seen in Niki Sandstrom's gray eyes was boring a deep black hole into Tanya's soul. The kind of black that went on forever without a light at the end of it. Black emptiness. Infinite black.

CHAPTER FIVE

ONCE TANYA WAS in the powder room, she locked herself in one of the small cubicles and sat down on the toilet lid. She suddenly felt weak and shaky.

It was over, she thought numbly. No point in fireworks. She had lost. And she loved Rafe too much to hurt him. Let him have his business. Let him have Niki. She sat in the cubicle for a long time, silently mourning the ashes of her marriage. She could not bring herself to go back into the ballroom. She just wanted to go home. Except her home was not her home anymore. It never really had been a home. Just a house. A beautiful empty house.

She thought of taking a taxi to her grandmother's home. But she couldn't turn up there in this dress. Her grandmother would probably die of shock. And she wouldn't approve of Tanya leaving Rafe. At least, though, she would listen. And she wouldn't turn her granddaughter away. *I'll go home to Grandma tomorrow,* Tanya thought. Tomorrow. Which left the problem of how to finish tonight.

A stirring of pride insisted that she see the night out with Rafe. That was what she had declared she would do. But he didn't want her at his side anymore. And she couldn't bear to watch Niki gloat. All the same, she couldn't just walk out on Rafe without saying goodbye. It wouldn't take long. He would let her go without any argument. He didn't want her anymore.

She felt cold and stiff as she pushed herself up from the toilet lid. Her fingers fumbled nervelessly on the door catch. A dull numbness spread through her mind. *They won't touch me,* Tanya thought. *Neither Niki nor Rafe. I'll just put them at a distance. Shut them out.*

She had reached the entrance to the ballroom when a hand from behind tapped her shoulder. Her head snapped around, her eyes flaring rejection in her need to be left alone to her own private misery. But when she saw the friendly grinning face of Harry Graham, she gradually relaxed into a responding smile.

Harry was a nice man. He was not particularly handsome, but he had the kind of face that invited trust, a kindly boy-next-door face, although he was well into his thirties. His dark brown eyes crinkled with good humor and his thick thatch of straight brown hair had a tendency to flop onto his forehead in a way that made women feel they wanted to brush it back for him. His grin was infectious.

Tanya had been one of his research assistants for his television chat show, before Rafe insisted on her throwing in the job to marry him. She hadn't seen Harry since, at least not in the flesh, but he had been a good boss, always appreciative of the staff who backed him up, and particularly nice to her.

"Hot stuff tonight, Tanya," he teased with an appreciative glance down at her dress. He wriggled his eyebrows—one of his on-camera trademarks. "I rather suspect there's not a man here who doesn't envy your husband. It must give him a lot of pleasure."

Not tonight, Harry, Tanya thought, but the comment on Rafe's kind of thinking was too accurate, too penetrating for her to answer. It reflected her position in Rafe's life too closely. Her ex-position.

She gave a short embarrassed laugh. Harry had been present at Tanya's first meeting with Rafe when he was an interviewee on Harry's show. Harry had teased her afterwards about Rafe being on fire at first sight, laughingly commenting that he had felt quite scorched just standing on the sidelines.

"Everything working out okay?" he asked.

"More or less," she said evenly, not wanting to discuss it. Then she remembered that Harry had been very recently divorced, a much publicized item in the gossip columns. "I'm sorry about Helen."

He shrugged. *"C'est la vie!"* he said, but there was a flash of bleak emptiness in his expressive brown eyes. "I guess I didn't treat her right," he added with dry humility.

I know what he's feeling, Tanya thought sympathetically. *That bleak emptiness is burrowing through me right now.* She remembered just how much Harry had idolized Helen for the strikingly beautiful woman she was. He had to be hurting very badly. As badly as Tanya was. According to the gossip columns, Helen had left him for a gorgeous hunk who happened to be a top male model. Tanya wondered why. The man apparently didn't have a brain in his head.

Sex, she supposed.

Like Rafe with her.

Tanya couldn't imagine a woman wanting to divorce Harry, but no one ever really knew what went on inside other people's marriages. Harry had seen and felt the sexual attraction between Tanya and Rafe, but he had no idea of the actual situation between them.

"So what are you up to?" he asked. "No family on the horizon as yet?"

Tanya's face tightened a little as she gave Rafe's usual reply. "Not yet."

"And you always led me to believe you were an old-fashioned girl who would have babies from ear to ear," Harry teased softly. "Wasn't that why you threw up your job with me?"

"Not really," Tanya returned lightly. "Rafe didn't want me to keep it on."

His eyebrows wagged. "Well, I guess you're fairly busy being Rafe's wife."

"It keeps me occupied," she agreed.

"So why do I get the feeling you're not very happy?" he asked, the brown eyes suddenly turning serious.

Before Tanya could think of a suitable reply, Harry's gaze flicked over her shoulder. "And why do I feel I'm about to be murdered? Don't look now, my sweet, but your husband is bearing down on us at a rate of knots with black thunderclouds rolling around his head and his eyes blazing like lightning bolts. Should I fade into the shadows or stand here like a gallant knight of old, protecting the fair maiden?"

Tanya's heart lurched. Had she blown the business deal that was so important to Rafe? She hadn't meant to. But if that had happened, would he believe her? The answer to that was quite obviously, no.

Harry heaved a sigh and flicked his gaze back to Tanya, a rueful sympathy in his eyes. "I think you're about to be murdered, too, so I'd better stay and stand guard."

"Harry—" her eyes begged his forbearance "—this is my fight, not yours. Thank you, but..."

"Not at all. My pleasure. Divorce tends to have a crippling effect upon one's manhood. Rafe is stirring it to life once more. I shall not skulk away like a coward. And you, my sweet, will show the backbone you always had. Quite unique in my experience. May I say what a vision of loveliness you are tonight. You should bare that backbone more often. Smile now. He's almost upon us. And we're both as innocent as babes."

He teased a shaky smile from her. But Harry had to be wrong about Rafe looking murderously at him. There was no point to jealousy anymore. Rafe had wiped her off. He didn't want a possession who got in his way. He particularly didn't want a possession who messed up his business.

"Graham..." came the icy acknowledgment from Rafe.

Tanya threw him an apprehensive glance. There was a white line around Rafe's mouth. His eyes seared her with white-hot heat. Her heart shriveled under their glare. Harry was right, she thought. Lightning bolts.

"Ah, the man himself!" Harry said with easy bonhomie, totally ignoring the instant thickening of the atmosphere around them. "Tanya was just telling me she's not in the family way yet," he burbled on. "So I was telling her if she ever wanted her old job back again, all she has to do is give me a call."

"Kind of you," Rafe clipped out, bored dismissal in his tone as he added, "but Tanya doesn't need a job. Now if you'd excuse us..."

The brown eyes speared down to Tanya's, sharply intent. "Think of me as a port in a storm. If you want shelter—"

"I shall look after *my wife,* Graham," Rafe sliced in with all the bite of a blizzard.

Pride, Tanya thought. Black pride. He didn't give a damn about her anymore, but it would spoil Rafe's image of himself if he didn't provide for her . . . either as his wife or ex-wife. Rafe would always pay for his mistakes. That was the cost of being taught not to repeat them.

Harry ignored him. "Tanya?"

She did not look up at Rafe but she was vibrantly aware of the violence emanating from his stiff unyielding body. He had to be in a towering fury. Even worse than when they had left home. It was crazy of Harry to involve himself. Gallant, though, and Tanya was deeply grateful for his job offer because she was not going to accept any support from Rafe.

"Thank you, Harry," she said softly. "And thank you for talking to me," she added in pointed dismissal. Harry was a nice man. Too nice to be caught in tonight's cross fire between her and Rafe.

He nodded acquiescence to her decision. "Au revoir, my sweet. Just remember . . . shipwrecks are my present specialty. I know all about them."

He lifted derisive eyes to Rafe. "He who does not value a jewel . . . is a fool."

Then he raised his hand in a mock salute and walked away.

Tanya took a deep breath to steady her quivering nerves, then turned to face Rafe. His gaze was following Harry and there was murder in his eyes. It be-

wildered Tanya for a moment. It couldn't be jealousy.
Then she recollected Harry's last mocking comment.
Rafe would hate being considered a fool by anyone.

Time to finish it, here and now, Tanya thought. At
least then it wouldn't be under Niki's eyes. "You
wanted me for something, Rafe?" she asked, drawing his fire back to her.

His face was so tight, the skin seemed to barely
stretch over his bones. His gaze flicked down to hers,
diamond-hard now, revealing nothing. "You were
gone a long time," he remarked flatly.

"You did tell me to go and enjoy myself," she reminded him.

His mouth took on a sardonic curl. "Perhaps I was
surprised by your wifely obedience. It was a little late
in coming tonight."

"I presume your perfect personal assistant is holding the fort while you came looking for your way-
ward wife," she snapped, unable to hold back a tide
of resentment at his manner towards her.

"I can rely on Niki, yes," he bit back coldly.

She *was* stupid, Tanya thought. A stupid masochist
for inviting more pain on top of the pain she already
had. She heaved a sigh to relieve the tight constriction
in her chest. "If it means anything to you, I'm sorry
for wearing this dress, Rafe," she said dully. "And
I'm sorry about Mr. Yorgansson."

"Mr.? Surely you reached more intimate terms than
that while you danced with him, Tanya," he drawled
sarcastically. "Yorgan is very eagerly awaiting your
return."

Tanya could feel the blood draining from her face.
Rafe couldn't mean he wanted her to go back and ac-

commodate his business target. He wouldn't use her like that, would he? Even though he felt nothing for her anymore, his business interests couldn't be that important to him. She was still *his wife*.

"I don't feel well," she stated shakily. "I was just coming to tell you that I think it best if I leave."

He raised his eyebrows. "Had enough blood for tonight, Tanya? And just when *I* was getting in the mood for it."

"A pity we can't get our timing better synchronized, isn't it?" she retorted on a burst of bitterness. "We might have done a lot better if we'd stayed at home."

"Undoubtedly," he agreed, a savage derision in his eyes. "Then I would still be as blind as ever about you."

"As opposed to being determinedly deaf and dumb about everything you don't want to acknowledge," she shot back at him, her chin lifting in defiant pride.

Bleak eyes met bleak, acknowledging the unbridgeable chasm between them.

Rafe shrugged. "Perhaps it is for the best if you leave. I might get some business done, after all."

"Yes. I thought you'd see it that way, Rafe," Tanya said with acid sweetness. "Oh, and do give my congratulations to your *other woman*. She knew you better than I did. Which, of course, is understandable. You've given her more of yourself than you've ever given me."

His lips thinned. His eyes blazed fire. He really hated her saying anything about his precious perfect Niki. Tanya hoped the venomous blonde was as cold in bed as her iceberg-gray eyes. Maybe Rafe would regret his choice then. Not that it would make any difference to Tanya. Her relationship with him was dead.

"I'll see you into a taxi," Rafe said tersely.

"There's no need."

"You're my wife," he grated.

"Oh, yes! Display purposes!" Tanya constructed an adoring look and flashed it at him as she stepped towards the elevators.

He muttered something savage under his breath and joined her, jabbing a finger at the down button as though he wished it was a destruct button. The doors opened with commendable swiftness. Rafe swept his arm around Tanya's waist and scooped her inside the compartment. It was not occupied by anyone else and no one else joined them. As the doors closed on them Tanya shut her eyes and fiercely, foolishly wished they could keep the rest of the world out forever. Then she and Rafe would always be together.

But it was only a few seconds before the doors opened onto the ground floor, a few seconds of intense awareness of what she had lost. *I hate him,* she told herself, but she knew it was a lie. She loved him. She loved him with all the desolation in her soul.

Oddly enough Rafe retained his arm around her waist as they walked down the long red carpet to the main foyer exit. His hold on her was a bittersweet torment to Tanya. She knew it had to be only a courtesy thing, yet despite everything, the warmth of his hand on her hip seeped into her blood, stirring the desire she had always felt with him.

Even the brush of his coat sleeve against her bare back sent electric goose bumps over her skin. She thought how madly ironic it was that Yorgan Yorgansson's subtle caresses could leave her absolutely cold, and Rafe's coat sleeve could arouse her to a pitch of awareness that had her nerves screaming for more and more of his touch.

The doorman opened the door for them. They were no sooner out in the forecourt than Rafe raised an arm to hail a taxi from the waiting line. Wanting to be rid of her as fast as possible, Tanya thought in wretched misery.

"I didn't bring any money with me, Rafe," she whispered, mortified at having to ask him for anything.

Without a word he reached inside his dinner jacket and handed her a slim billfold of hundred-dollar notes. When it came to money, there was nothing mean about Rafe Carlton. It was only himself he never gave.

"Thank you," she murmured, flushing with painful embarrassment as she hastily shoved the billfold into her evening bag. It was the last thing she would ever ask of him.

The taxi pulled up in front of them and Rafe stepped away from her to open the passenger door. Tanya realized then there was one more thing she wanted to ask of Rafe. She paused beside him, looking up into his grim stony face. His eyes held no softness for her. Nothing but bleak determination to have it finished.

She swallowed hard to work some moisture into her mouth, which had gone impossibly dry. What did it matter if he rejected her request? Suddenly pride meant nothing at all. She ran her tongue around her numb lips, wanting to put some feeling into them.

The action drew Rafe's gaze momentarily. Then his mouth thinned and his eyes flicked back to hers, harder than ever. "Do you need anything else?" he asked, a raw gravelly tone in his voice.

Harsh.

Harsh and brusque.

Now or never, Tanya urged herself. "Will you kiss me goodbye, Rafe?" Her voice was a bare husky whisper.

He looked as though he was going to refuse. Angry impatience flitted over his face. Then a dry mockery settled in his eyes. "Of course," he said.

He leaned over and brushed his lips against hers, a touch so brief it was virtually a studied insult. Tanya barely felt the contact before it was gone, leaving her feeling so bereft that tears welled into her eyes. She turned blindly and stepped into the taxi. The door was firmly closed after her. She blinked hard, looked out the side window, saw that Rafe had already turned away. . . a dynamic black figure striding quickly and purposefully down the red carpet again.

Going back to Niki.

"Where to, lady?" the taxi driver asked.

Where to?

It was a good question.

Tanya struggled to find an answer.

She remembered the money in her bag. Plenty of money. A means to an end. The end of her marriage to Rafe.

"The Sebel Town House," she replied wearily.

It was a good hotel, and on the way to Potts Point. It was also out of the central city district. There would be very few people around there in the morning to raise their eyebrows at seeing her emerge in this disastrous black dress to catch a taxi home.

Rafe would be gone to work by eight o'clock. He always was. Tomorrow would not be any different. She would be packed and gone by the time he returned home in the evening. She didn't want to see him again. Ever. There was nothing left now. Nothing. Only the ashes in her heart.

The fire was out.

CHAPTER SIX

TANYA DIDN'T GET much sleep. It was the first time she had slept alone in a bed since marrying Rafe. She told herself that she had to start getting used to it, but she was tortured by a continual sequence of far too vivid memories.

She ordered breakfast in her room and picked at it, more for something to do, to pass the time, than from any need for food. She had no appetite. She felt ill, although there was nothing physically wrong with her. It would pass, she told herself. All things passed in time. So people said. She wondered if they were right because she couldn't imagine feeling worse than she did right now.

She kept watching the digits change on the clock radio beside the bed. When the numbers read 8:05 she called reception to organize an instant checkout. Five minutes, she was assured. Five minutes of squirming embarrassment, Tanya thought.

She felt extremely self-conscious about wearing the black dress out in broad daylight. What a mistake that had been, she thought miserably. But at the present moment, she no longer had any choice. To make matters worse, the spectacle she would make in her dress was further compounded by the tangled mess of her hair. She needed a brush to make any order of it and she simply didn't have one. All she could do was limit her visibility as much as possible.

This would never have happened to Niki Sandstrom, Tanya thought. She would have planned her retreat down to the last degree. Tanya couldn't imagine the supercool blonde reacting as emotionally as she had. No, Niki wouldn't have a hair out of place.

Tanya wondered if she made love with the same smooth precision. Had Rafe bothered to go home last night or had his ever-ready assistant persuaded him to find consolation with her? No, Rafe wouldn't be persuaded into anything he didn't want to do. If he stayed with her, it was because he *decided* to do it.

Either way, he wouldn't be home now, Tanya assured herself. Rafe always left at eight o'clock on the dot. Not quite always, Tanya amended. But this morning she wasn't there to tempt him into any semblance of unpunctuality. So he wouldn't be there.

Tanya screwed up her courage and left the room to go down to reception. Five excruciating minutes later she was stepping into a taxi. She gave the Potts Point address to the driver and settled back in the seat with a little sigh of relief. Then the unbidden thought came that wherever she went, life was going to be very empty. Rafe would never be there for her again. His goodbye kiss had told her that.

For the first time her resolve wavered. Had she been mad to walk away from Rafe? The memories of what caused that decision came slowly back. She had no choice. Otherwise, for the rest of her life she would be treated like a performing doll. Somewhere there had to be a meeting of minds between Rafe and her. With his attitudes, that was not about to happen. No matter how much it hurt, she had to go her own way.

With her mind revolving around issues and counterissues, the trip did not seem to take long, even though the roads were clogged with peak-hour traffic. As the taxi pulled up outside the house Tanya noted that the Aston Martin was not in the driveway. The garage doors were shut but she was certain that Rafe's car would not be there either. It was eight-thirty. She paid off the taxi driver then hurried up the path to the front door.

She didn't pause to admire the impressive lines of the two-story white house, or the landscaped grounds, or the harbor view. They had all been meaningless for a long time now. Stage props to a wealthy marriage. Except the wealth was all external and a symbol of Rafe's material success.

Tanya paused only to pick up the emergency house key from the potted plant near the steps. She jammed it in the front door, anxious to get inside, out of sight of any curious eyes. It was a relief to close the door behind her, to know she was finally here to do what had to be done and to make her private farewells to memories.

For a private home, the foyer was spacious and elegant. Doors led off from either side, to the formal lounge room on the left, and to the more casual living room on the right. Facing her was the wide imposing staircase that led up to the bedrooms.

Change out of this dress first, Tanya thought, and headed straight for the stairs, her high heels clacking on the tiled floor. Her hand was on the banister, one foot lifted on the first step when she was halted by Rafe's voice.

"So...the cat has finally come home!"

It was a slow derisive drawl that punched into her heart and sent a frisson of shock down her spine. She swung around, instinctively reaching out to hold on to the banister again to steady herself. Rafe was standing in the doorway to the living room, lounging there in a lazy indolent pose, his back against the doorjamb, arms akimbo.

He still wore the black trousers of his dress suit, but the jacket and bow tie had long been discarded. His shirt gaped half-open and the sleeves were rolled up his forearms. His jaw was darkly shadowed, unshaved. His thick black hair was mussed. There was a weary washed-out look around his eyes, but the blue irises were blazing, more vivid than ever. Electric blue. Stabbing at her with intense bitterness.

His relaxed pose was a sham. He looked like a dangerous wild animal, waiting its chance to pounce. And it wouldn't end with pouncing. He wanted to claw and rip and shred and devour. The pulse in his throat was throbbing. The muscles in his forearms were taut and threatening. An aura of barely suppressed violence shimmered around him.

Tanya's mind was totally blank. He wasn't supposed to be here. She stared at him, mesmerized by all the signs that the fire wasn't out. Not yet. Not until she was consumed to his satisfaction.

"Nothing to say, Tanya?" he mocked. "No explanation? No excuses? No friendly greeting this fine morning?"

Her fingers stretched around the banister, gripping hard. Her legs seemed to have lost all substance and she needed the support. Her heart had gone mad, hammering as though it would pound her to death, and her stomach was turning inside out. Her mind whirred with activity, trying to fathom Rafe. In the end, all she could manage was the question uppermost in a chaos of questions.

"What are you doing here?" Her voice sounded disembodied, even to her.

"Waiting for you," he said grimly, almost spitting the words out.

He had never waited for her before. For Rafe that had to be a new experience. He didn't like it. "I expected you to have gone to work," she said by way of explanation and apology, although she didn't even understand herself why she should apologize. "But you're here," she added weakly.

"Yes. I'm here. I've been here for nine hours and twenty-three minutes," he stated with savage emphasis. "Did you have a good time, Tanya? Whom did you *ravish?*"

"Don't be stupid, Rafe!" she shot at him, flushing at the memory of what she had said about wanting to be ravished last night. But Rafe hadn't wanted her then as she had wanted him.

His mouth curled thinly. "You were out for blood, Tanya. And you got it."

She stared at him incredulously. He couldn't believe she had gone off with someone else. He had seen her into the taxi. "For God's sake, Rafe! That's absurd...."

"Is it, Tanya? Then why didn't you come home?"

Her chin went up. He was not the only one whose pride had been wounded. "Your goodbye kiss last night was supremely indifferent."

"Oh! So everything hinged on that, did it?"

"Not *everything*."

"How unfair you are, Tanya!" His back came off the doorjamb. His arms swung loosely at his sides as he strolled towards her, every lazy step a statement of absolute confidence. His voice dripped sweet acid, each drop designed to burn into her mind and heart and soul.

"A pity you didn't tell me that your fidelity and loyalty to me hung on the way I kissed you in public. If I'd known that, I might have given you a more... testing... performance."

Her eyes flared with bitterness. "I didn't want a performance, Rafe. I've had enough *performances* to last me the rest of my life."

"So who provided what I didn't give you, Tanya?" he drove back at her in relentless purpose. "Was it Graham? Or our good friend, Yorgansson? Oh, I'm a lucky man to have such a jewel, aren't I? A jewel that can attract any man she fancies. So who was it, Tanya? Just for the record..."

"You're mad," she whispered, horrified that he could think she had gone to either man. Any other man!

"Not mad, Tanya," he drawled. "I doubt anyone would believe that."

She shook her head in dismay. Why should Rafe believe such wicked things about her? Yorgan Yorgansson was virtually a stranger. Harry... Rafe knew she had worked for Harry for years and there had

never been anything but a friendly association between them. Besides, what she had given Rafe was for
him alone, not something that could ever be shared
with someone else. Surely he knew that. He had to
know that about her, at the very least! Or did he
equate her with sex so much that he couldn't think of
her in any other terms?

He reached her, placed his hand over hers on the
banister, trapping it there, then lifted his other hand
to stroke the dimple in her chin with a softly teasing
finger. His eyes glittered a deadly challenge.
"So...what I want to know is," he said silkily, "are
you satisfied now?"

"No, Rafe." She looked at him despairingly.
"Whatever I do, I don't ever think like that."

"What a pity!" He forced his face into a grimace of
a smile. "See how understanding I am of my little
wife's needs? How very sane and understanding?
Forgiving might take a little longer. I'm not very good
at that...but who knows?" His fingers dropped to the
front slit in her dress and ran slowly down her cleavage. "There are times when you can make me forget
anything."

He wanted her. He *still* wanted her. A turbulent
confusion shook her entire body. Or was Rafe lying?
Taunting her? Taking some malicious revenge for her
behavior last night? Had he lost the deal he'd wanted?
Because of her?

His finger left a trail of prickling sensitivity on her
skin. He picked it away from the end of the slit, then
lifted his hand to her hair, fanning it out through his
fingers.

"It must have been a wild tumble last night. You might have tried tidying up the evidence before you came home, Tanya," he chided. "A useless nicety, I suppose, but people might see and jump to valid conclusions. A man prefers these little considerations. A matter of pride. And it helps to dampen his imagination."

"Stop it, Rafe," she choked out, a little frightened by the intensity emanating from him.

"I'd like to stop it, Tanya. I really would. I've tried. But I can't do it. I've been wondering all night whom you chose to put in my place. How your body was responding to his. Whether you were making love to him—as you did with me last night—or whether you just let him make love to you. So it'd only be a kindness to settle the question for me. It would help put my fevered imaginings to rest. Graham or Yorgansson, Tanya?"

"Neither! Neither!" she croaked in sheer outrage that he should believe such a thing of her.

His eyebrows lifted in scornful disbelief. "So what did you do? Cruise around in a taxi until you spotted someone you fancied? Or did you take on the taxi driver?"

"I didn't!" she spit at him furiously. "I wasn't with anyone else! I went to the Sebel Town House and stayed the night there. I didn't think—"

He cut her off with a harsh laugh. "How convenient! Precisely where our friend Yorgansson is staying. Did you arrange it while you danced? I'd like to know just how double-faced he was when he spoke to me afterwards."

"I didn't arrange anything!" she denied, heaving for breath as the constriction in her chest tightened, squeezing her heart into pumping even more madly.

"Of course! I'm not thinking straight, am I? You have that effect on me, Tanya." His hand burrowed under her hair and began caressing the nape of her neck, his fingers moving in a soft kneading pattern. "It was after the goodbye kiss that you made up your mind—" his hot gaze dropped to her mouth and flicked up again in taunting mockery "—when I didn't display the fervor of a besotted man whom you could twist around your finger. Therefore, Yorgansson didn't know he'd struck the jackpot until after he got back to his hotel."

He wasn't listening. He never listened to her! She tried again, her voice trembling with furious resentment. "Rafe, I told you—"

"Where did he start, Tanya? Your breasts?" He dragged his hand from under her hair and started rotating his palm over her nipples. "You like that, don't you? You've always liked that," he purred, his eyes simmering into hers, waiting for the telltale response.

She couldn't stop her body from responding, and the wild glitter of triumph in his eyes curdled her stomach. "No, Rafe," she pleaded. "Not like this."

He deliberately misinterpreted her. "You're right. It's better without clothes, isn't it?" he hissed.

Her glazed mind couldn't think of any response. She wanted this ugly scene over, to be able to lean towards Rafe, press her body to his and forget everything else in the lovemaking he did so well.

His hands moved to the edges of the slit in her bodice. His mouth thinned with some grim satisfaction.

There was a flare of uncontrolled ferocity in his eyes. He yanked hard, tearing the fabric apart, rending the front seam right down through the hem of the skirt. The whole front of her dress hung in two sections, only joined by the high banded collar around her neck.

"I never thought that dress suited you all that well, Tanya," he remarked harshly. He stared down at her nakedness and groaned.

Tanya just stood there in quivering shock as he pushed the fabric aside and cupped her breasts in his hands.

"God knows you are beautiful!" he said in a raw frenzy of passion. "I can't blame any man for being fascinated by your shape. By the feel of you..." His hands moved down her body, touching her all over.

Tanya slapped him. She hadn't even known she had lifted her hand, or that she'd swung it so hard until it hit his face with a resounding crack and left her palm smarting painfully. She stared at him with wild eyes as the white imprint of her hand on his cheek slowly stained with red.

"Don't...you...touch...me," she panted, her chest heaving for breath. Then in one final explosive effort. "Ever again!"

A dark rumble issued from his throat. His eyes flamed with a violent glitter. His hands shot out and grabbed her. He hoisted her over his shoulder and charged up the stairs. Tanya tried to kick. He fastened his arms more tightly around her thighs. Her hands flayed his back but he seemed insensitive to any pain she could inflict. A seething torrent of fury poured from him as he charged on.

"Not touch you! Goddamned little bitch! Not touch you! You wanted me to touch you last night! All night! And because I didn't...because I put something else ahead of your whims and desires...you put me through a night of pure hell! Letting some other man touch you!"

He kicked aside the bedroom door, venting violence on that before striding over the bed and tipping her onto it. He knelt on the remnants of her dress, pinning her down as he tore off his shirt, still spitting rage.

"You're nothing but a witch! Driving every man to get the hots for you. And then telling me I can't touch you! Not touch you! When you let every other Tom, Dick and Harry touch you! Like hell I can't touch you!"

He unfastened his trousers and shoved them down his hips. "Don't you move!" he threatened as he stood up to throw them off. "I'm going to touch you. I'm going to touch you like you've never been touched before. And when I'm finished, you'll damned well know whose woman you are. You're *mine!*"

Tanya didn't move. It was not Rafe's determination that held her still. It was the mesmerising fascination of seeing him out of control. Totally out of control.

It had never happened before. The realization that he had tortured himself all night with visions of her making love with some other man was filtering through her shocked mind. She had completely misunderstood his manner towards her. He had been exerting control. That was all gone now.

She should have been frightened, but she wasn't. There was something excitingly primitive about Rafe's seething aggression. She wanted him. Just like this. Out of control. And he wanted her. His whole body was taut with his need to take her, to possess her with a domination that would forever stamp his brand on her. It was in his eyes, on his face, in the heaving turmoil that pulsed through the sharply delineated muscles of his chest, in the swollen erection of his manhood and in the tightly corded muscles of his powerful thighs as he knelt on the bed and pulled her legs around him.

"You're *mine!* Not anyone else's!" he claimed, a fierce animal possessiveness in his voice as he drove himself into her. Tanya felt a fiercely primitive exultation. Yes, she was his. But not in the way Rafe thought she was.

Gone was the knowing expertise of the lover she had known. Gone was the conscious care for her pleasure. Gone was the controlled escalation to climax. He ravaged her, possessing her like a wild bull with his own pounding need to eliminate any other man but him, to own her with obsessive totality. And Tanya gloried in every wild moment of it. Rafe . . . out of control.

She didn't care what he did . . . how he used her. For this one time only Rafe was hers, and hers alone. He wasn't thinking of business. He wasn't thinking of Niki. He was hers. He was all hers in those mind-smashing plunges that took him deep inside her . . . so exquisitely deep that her flesh seemed to mesh with his, drawing from it, engulfing it, contracting around it in storm-tossed waves that beat and pulverized and shattered any other existence. And she knew that he was also mindless this time...and only she existed for him. Only she. Possessing him.

He cried her name in hoarse need—or despair—as he spilled himself into her, and she felt the hot liquid sensation of melting around him, loving him, wanting him to love her.

But he didn't.

She was totally limp; beyond movement, beyond speech, beyond thought. She watched him through her thick lashes, waiting...waiting for him to move towards her or away.

Hold me, Rafe, she willed silently. *Hold me close.*

But he didn't. He moved away, and Tanya saw the dawning of an incredulous horror in his eyes as he looked down at her. Anguish twisted his face. He completely withdrew, putting her from him in hurried movements that had a guilty gentleness and an inward revulsion.

Tanya knew intuitively that he hated himself for his loss of control, hated what he'd done, was totally appalled that he could have been drawn into such raw animalism. He sat on the side of the bed, his elbows on his knees, his head in his hands. Not indomitable Rafe at all. Hurting Rafe. For the first time in all her experience with him, he looked heart-wrenchingly vulnerable.

She almost spoke.

The words hovered on her tongue. *It doesn't matter. You needed to do it. I liked having you feel that. I didn't have another man. I love you.*

Then he seemed to give himself a shake and stood up. He squared his shoulders as though to prepare for taking up the burdens of his life again. Indomitable

Rafe. He walked over to the wall cupboards, collected a clean set of clothes, headed for the bathroom...like a robot, mechanically going through routine motions...orderly, precise, controlled.

The door closed behind him, shutting her out.

Tanya slowly rolled onto her side, turning her back to the bathroom door. She pulled a loose section of her torn dress over her nakedness. Tears welled into her eyes and overflowed. Impossible to stop them. She knew what Rafe was doing. He was washing her off him. Cleaning himself up for business as usual. With Niki.

Nothing was going to change. No, that was wrong. There could be a change. In future, Rafe would be more controlled than ever. Unbreakable.

A numb haze spread across Tanya's mind, filtered through her body. Tears kept spilling down her cheeks but it was a silent crying. She didn't move. She didn't make a sound. The crying was deep inside her.

She heard Rafe emerge from the bathroom, knew that he stood looking at her for a long time. It seemed to go on forever. She felt his guilt, his uncertainty, his remorse. But he didn't love her. He hated himself.

Finally he walked over to the bed, sat down on the other side where he didn't have to look at her face. He leaned over, stroked her hair. Very softly.

"Did I hurt you, Tanya?" he asked in a low voice, almost unrecognizable as his.

Yes. My heart is breaking, she thought. She swallowed the lump in her throat and said, "No."

He kept on stroking.

She didn't move.

"I'm sorry." The words were low and gruff, edged with pain.

"You really believe I had another man last night?" she asked dully.

There was a long pause before he answered. He stopped stroking her hair, withdrew his touch. "The thought crossed my mind...."

"I didn't, Rafe." Flat denial. Take it or leave it. It didn't really matter anymore. Nothing mattered much anymore.

"Tanya..." Pain...diluted by a heavy sigh. His hand curved gently around her shoulder. "What can I do?"

"Go to work, Rafe. That's what you want to do," she said in weary resignation.

His fingers moved back and forth over her shoulder, revealing his agitation of mind—whether to go or whether to stay. Finally he took a firmer grip to draw her over onto her back. Tanya didn't resist. She didn't have the energy to resist. Nor did she have the will. If Rafe wanted to look at her, let him look. It would be the last time.

The tears had stopped, but wetness still clung to her lashes and the damp trails on her cheeks were clear evidence of her distress. She looked up at him with bleak empty eyes, uncaring of her appearance, expecting nothing of him.

He looked at her strangely, as though seeing a different person from the Tanya he had married. Which she was, of course, from his point of view. An unfaithful wife was a lot different from an untouched virgin.

He looked different, too. Somehow older. His face harshly etched. But that was probably from lack of sleep.

"I think it's better if I stay with you," he said.

She turned her head away, rejecting his guilt. Or sympathy. Or whatever had prompted his offer. "No, Rafe," she sighed. Her chest wasn't tight anymore but it felt very heavy. Her heart seemed to be pumping to a slow dull thud. A death knell, she thought, as she added, "I want to be alone. For a while. To sort out my thoughts."

"I'd rather..."

"Oh, for God's sake, go!" she broke in with a sudden burst of anger. "After what you just put me through, I want to be alone."

"All right," he said heavily, then with an edge of doubt, "if that's what you want."

A hysterical bubble rose in her throat and she swallowed it back down. It was the last thing she wanted, but what she did want, Rafe couldn't—wouldn't—give her. There was nothing to talk about. How could they talk about it? Would Rafe ever believe that she had spent last night alone?

Besides, she had all her answers now. Nothing was going to change. Rafe hadn't listened to her last night, and he certainly hadn't listened to her this morning. He was never going to listen to anything that went against what *he* thought.

"Go," she said flatly.

Still he hesitated. "Will you be all right?" he asked, a gravelled note of concern in his voice.

"Yes."

He paused a few moments longer, then said, "I won't be late home."

Tanya made no reply. It didn't matter if he was late or not. She wouldn't be here.

He left.

She waited until she heard the thrum of the Aston Martin pulling out of the driveway. She didn't want to move. It was difficult to push herself out of her cocoon of misery. But she had to. There was nothing to be gained by wallowing in desolation. One step at a time, she told herself. She had to walk away from all this by the end of the day.

Tanya did not pack all the clothes that Rafe had bought for her. She didn't need them for the life-style she was returning to, and it didn't seem right to take them anyway. Nor did she take the jewelry he had given her. Baubles for his parakeet.

When she was cleaning her things out of the bathroom, she realized she had missed taking a contraceptive pill last night. She quickly swallowed one down. It was twelve hours late but she doubted it would matter. In fact, it was probably silly taking it at all. Except she would get her period if she didn't. Better to finish off the month's supply. She wouldn't need to worry about taking pills after that.

By early afternoon she had completed her packing and tidied the house. She wondered if Rafe would keep on the house after she was gone. Probably not, she decided. He would undoubtedly make a lot of money on it by selling. And Niki certainly wouldn't want to live anywhere that had any memories of Tanya.

Before ringing for a taxi to take her to her grandmother's, Tanya sat down to write Rafe a letter. She hadn't meant to put him through hell last night, and she didn't want to put him through any more. She just wanted a clean break. It was better for both of them. Particularly after this morning.

She decided on a brief note. No emotion. After all, their marriage had only been about sex. So she wrote:

Dear Rafe,
I don't want to live with you anymore. I'm going back to my grandmother's home. I don't want any money from you. I can support myself. I intend to pick up my life again, as it was before I met you. I wish you every happiness in whatever you choose to do. I'm sorry, but I don't want to be part of it ever again. Thank you for giving me what you have.

                                        Tanya

She propped the note against the pillows on their bed. It seemed like the most appropriate place. She walked through the rooms of the house once more; rooms she had decorated with love in her heart and hope for the future. But there was no love. No hope.

Finally she called for a taxi.

She left the house that Rafe had bought her without a backward glance, determined not to regret what she was doing. She was a person, not a sex object or a possession to be owned and displayed. She was a person who had more value than that. She was only twenty-three years old. She had a long life ahead of her. She blinked back the tears. Regrets were a waste of time.

CHAPTER SEVEN

THE TAXI DRIVER deposited Tanya's bags on the pavement in front of her grandmother's home and drove away. Tanya took a few moments to compose herself before facing the woman who had brought her up. Grandma was going to be disappointed in her. To Bea Wakefield, a commitment was a commitment. Giving up was unthinkable. But giving in was unthinkable too, Tanya argued to herself, and somehow she had to make Grandma understand that.

There was a stark uniformity about all the houses in this respectable street of the north-shore suburb of Artarmon. Every one was of dark red brick. Each had a gabled "front" room to one side, and a porch that extended across the remaining face of the house. Yet Bea Wakefield's house was set apart from the rest, like a beacon of brightness and beauty among the uniform drabness.

Flowers bloomed on every available inch of it; bursting from the small front yard, trailing all over the wall of the front porch, hanging from the rafters. They lifted the house out of the ordinary, and although Bea Wakefield would never have had such a thought, the extraordinary show of magnificent blooms was a reflection of her extraordinary character; determined, resourceful, dedicated to making the best of what she had. But it also meant a lot of caring as well, Tanya assured herself.

The flowers looked particularly bright and welcoming to her as she unlatched the front gate. *Grandma's been at the Vegemite jar again,* she thought. A long time ago, when money was very tight, Bea had figured out that if eating Vegemite was supposed to make children grow, why shouldn't it make plants and flowers grow as well? She had mixed some with water, fed it to some sick-looking geraniums, and the results had been astonishing.

Over later years, when Bea could afford to try fancy manures and fertilizers on her garden, she found that nothing beat her Vegemite. Tanya had discovered her grandmother making up this magical formula when she was a little girl, and had been sworn to eternal silence. After all, if everyone knew how Grandma grew championship flowers, everyone else could do the same.

In fact, there was very little money involved in the richness of Grandma's garden. Practically everything had been grown from cuttings or bulbs that had been given to her, and she simply lavished a lot of care on them. Money couldn't buy that kind of care.

It was the kind of care Tanya had missed in her marriage to Rafe. The care that nurtured and made things grow and become better and better all the time. There had been no growing in her relationship with Rafe. If anything, it had become stunted through lack of feeding, or lack of care.

Tanya heaved a weary sigh. She hoped Grandma would understand that she had not left Rafe lightly. The problems in their marriage were too deep and endemic for ready solutions to be found. It was not that she didn't love him—she would always love him—but she just couldn't live with him anymore. It was destroying her.

She lugged the suitcases up the steps to the porch. They were heavy but not as heavy as her heart. She rang the doorbell. Her grandmother was not long in answering the summons, and somehow it was an enormous relief for Tanya to see her again.

Bea Wakefield was a strong woman. Even at seventy years of age, her tall large-framed figure was totally undiminished. She stood tall. Every bit as indomitable as Rafe. Not even her deep bosom was allowed to sag. Her once-red hair was now pure white, but still as thick as ever. Unlike Tanya's wild cloud, it was tamed into a short layered cut that neatly framed her face. It was a face that had known sorrow and sadness and risen above both; full of character lines that warned she had seen a great deal of life, knew right from wrong, knew the good from the bad, knew precisely how to handle every situation and tolerated no nonsense.

But there was kindness there as well. Kindness and generosity. Tanya couldn't remember anyone ever asking her grandmother for help and being turned away. Except about her secret with the Vegemite. But that was a matter of personal pride, and not really important to anyone else's well-being.

Her bright hazel eyes widened in surprise at seeing Tanya, then swiftly narrowed as they caught the signs of strain and distress on her granddaughter's face. She took in the luggage with a cursory glance, then stepped forward and drew Tanya into a close embrace, nestling her against her ample bosom and holding her tight.

This is what love is all about, Rafe, Tanya thought savagely. *This is real caring.* She wrapped her arms around her grandmother, hugging her back fiercely. "It's good to see you, Grandma," she said huskily, and kissed her cheek in a flood of deep affection.

Bea Wakefield leaned back, a slight smile playing upon her face. "And it's always lovely to see you, Tanya." She considered for a moment, looked Tanya in the eyes and said, "So we had better go inside and I'll make you a cup of tea."

"That would be nice, Grandma." There was a slight quiver in her voice.

"And then you can tell me all your problems."

"How..." Rafe couldn't have rung. He couldn't even know about her defection yet.

"My dear..." Bea Wakefield gave her reassuring, everything-will-be-all-right hug. Over the years she had had a lot of practice with her granddaughter and she was very good at it. Then she eyed Tanya with that dry, contained, almost amused look. "As a rule of thumb, and as a guideline to life, you can always believe this: when people come calling on you with two suitcases of luggage, they have a problem."

"I..." Tanya swallowed hard. Her green eyes filled with vulnerable appeal. "I've come home, Grandma."

"You're always welcome here, my dear," came the reassuring reply. "Now let's get inside and be comfortable about it."

For the rest of the afternoon they sat in the straight-backed chairs on either side of the heavy oak table in the dining room, drinking the occasional cup of tea—

Bea Wakefield's panacea for all ills—while Tanya struggled to communicate her problem.

Explaining why she had walked away from Rafe was more difficult than she had realized. Rafe's excluding her from his business life, his refusal to consider having a baby, his attachment to Niki Sandstrom, Niki's all-too-intimate place at his side, the way they shut Tanya out…those things weren't too hard to say. But there were aspects of her relationship with Rafe that she could not possibly tell her grandmother, no matter how loving and concerned her grandmother was. They were things that she could not expect Grandma to understand. Like what happened in bed.

And to relate what had happened last night, or this morning, was equally impossible. Those crisis actions were too close to the bone for an airing to anyone else. Besides which, Grandma couldn't possibly understand them, either. It would only tarnish her opinion of both of them. Which apparently was already tarnished. Grandma didn't voice or show any overt disapproval, but Tanya could feel the ground swell of things unspoken.

"So I did the right thing…the only thing in the circumstances…didn't I, Grandma?" she asked tentatively, when there was no more that could be told.

"If you think so, dear." No outright approval. No outright rejection, either.

"What would you have done, Grandma?" Tanya persisted, trying to pin her down, wanting to make her see that she had done right.

"What I would have done doesn't really matter, Tanya," came the mild and determinedly evasive answer.

Tanya shook her head in frustration. Sometimes Grandma could be just like Rafe. In fact, in some things they were two of a kind. Unshakable. Always in control. Tanya felt a fierce stab of gladness that she had shaken Rafe out of his control this morning. At least she had won once. Even though in winning she had lost.

"Rafe only ever wanted me, Grandma," she said, needing to feel justified.

Her grandmother paused, as if for reflection, but there was a twinkle in her eyes, almost a suppressed smile. "Yes," she said dryly. "Men are like that. History teaches us that nothing has changed over the milleniums."

"But it shouldn't be like that!" Tanya cried in agonized protest.

"I agree."

A glitter of primitive ferocity leaped into Tanya's eyes. "So what's he doing to Niki Sandstrom?" she seethed.

"That's one of the questions I shall certainly ask Rafe when I see him."

"You think he'll come after me?" It was a question of hope and despair. Tanya both wanted him to, and wanted him to accept her decision and stay away.

"Oh yes," her grandmother said confidently. "I expect to hear from Rafe."

Which was more than Tanya expected.

The telephone rang and Bea rose to answer it. Tanya sat on at the table, sunk in despondent gloom. It was not until she heard her grandmother say, "Yes, she's here," that her ears pricked up. "And she's quite safe."

Only one person could be asking her grandmother about her. Rafe! She glanced at the grandfather clock next to the dresser. It was five-thirty. Rafe was not usually home until six, yet he wouldn't be ringing here unless he had read her note. He must have left work early today. Left Niki early. Guilt, Tanya surmised. He was probably still hating himself for what he'd done this morning. But that would pass soon, with not having to look at her anymore.

"As well as can be expected in the circumstances," her grandmother said.

Oh, yes, I'm all right, Rafe, Tanya thought savagely. *Blooming with health, without you to beat me down with your brand of possessiveness.*

Her grandmother shot her a questioning look then covered the telephone with her hand. "Do you want to speak to him?"

Tanya shook her head.

"No. She doesn't want to speak to you, Rafe."

Another silence, another questioning look, another covering of the telephone, another inquiry. "Can he come around?"

Again Tanya shook her head. As far as she was concerned, her letter had said it all. There was nothing to discuss.

"No. She doesn't want to see you, Rafe."

More silence. Then at last, "It's no good asking me, Rafe. You'll have to find out for yourself." End of conversation. "Goodbye." The telephone was replaced.

Her grandmother's bright hazel eyes had a distinctly speculative look as they scanned Tanya's mutinous face. "That was Rafe," she said unnecessarily.

"How is he?" Tanya returned, succumbing to a prick of curiosity.

"He didn't tell me," came the bland reply.

Tanya grimaced in frustration. "Well, what did he say, Grandma?"

"Hello. Wife missing. Was she here? Was..."

"I mean what's he going to do?" Tanya broke in impatiently.

Bea Wakefield assumed her most patient look. "Tanya, I was only answering the telephone. If you want to find out these things, you have to ask him yourself."

"Is he coming after me?" Tanya pressed.

"My dear, I'm sorry. I have no idea."

Of course he wasn't, Tanya told herself savagely. Why should he? A sexual obsession, that was all she had ever been to him. And now even that was over. It had been well and truly worked out of his system this morning. Rafe hadn't wanted to look at her after that.

Niki would get him now. When it came right down to the bottom line... Tanya had never really had him. He had been Niki's man all along.

Her grandmother jolted Tanya out of her dark introspection by placing a basket of peaches on the table in front of her. "Would you mind peeling these while I get dinner ready, Tanya?" she asked. "You know how I love stewed peaches."

"Of course, Grandma," Tanya muttered automatically.

It kept her busy for quite some time. She had just finished the task when the doorbell rang. Her grandmother went to answer the summons. Tanya ran the tap in the kitchen sink and washed the sticky fruit juice from her hands.

She didn't even wonder who the caller was. She had dismissed any notion that Rafe might come after her. It didn't make sense for him to do so. Her grandmother returned as Tanya was wiping her hands dry on the dish towel.

"That was Rafe," she announced matter-of-factly. "He's in the sitting room."

Tanya's heart catapulted around her chest. She stared incredulously at her grandmother. "Why?" The word tripped off her tongue, spilling from the turbulence that Rafe's visit poured through her mind.

"Ask him. He is your husband, Tanya," came the pointed reminder.

Her hands felt clammy. She wiped them on the towel again. Little shivers ran up and down her spine. She felt both hot and cold. And frightened. Because it meant so much . . . just to see him.

She savagely berated herself as she forced her legs to walk through the dining room and down the hallway to the sitting room. Rafe's coming here didn't mean anything. A duty visit. That was all. Discharging his sense of responsibility. Reinstating his control. His authority. It didn't mean he cared for her. He just couldn't abide her having the last word. He never had taken any notice of what she wanted.

The door had been left open. Rafe hadn't sat down. He stood in the middle of the room, waiting, watching for her to appear. Magnetic Rafe. So heart-wrenchingly handsome. Impeccably dressed in his navy-blue business suit. Classic silk tie—tiny navy anchors on red. Tanya had bought that tie for him. Did Rafe remember?

His face gave so little away. A mask of taut reserve. His blue eyes were dark. Very dark. They bored into Tanya with a kind of relentless directness, as though he was determined not to waver in whatever resolution he had in mind. No smile for her tonight. Tension flowed from him, swirled around her, making her achingly conscious of what had happened between them this morning.

Her mouth was a dry desert. She swallowed convulsively, working some moisture into it. Her chin tilted in defiant pride. "You didn't have to come," she stated belligerently.

"I wanted to," he replied, his voice soft and even . . . perfectly controlled.

"You always have to have your own way, don't you, Rafe?" she mocked bitterly.

A muscle in his cheek flinched. His whole jawline tightened as though he was clenching his teeth. "No, Tanya," he forced out quietly. "I'm sorry that you think that way. I'm sorry that I . . . forced myself on you. As I did. And I give you my word that I'll never treat you like that again."

"Like what, Rafe?" she retorted wearily. "A thing? That's nothing new. Just a bit more extreme than usual. I've only ever been a thing to you."

His chest rose and fell very slowly, almost as though he was deliberately pacing a long, long breath. When he spoke again it was in a slow measured tone. "I know you're upset, Tanya. And you have every right to be upset. But what you just said . . . that isn't fair."

"You've used me for the last time, Rafe," she said slowly, haltingly, meaningfully.

His head jerked back. His eyes seared hers with a wild burning torment. "I don't accept that I use you, Tanya. I've never used you. Not even this morning was I using you. I wanted you...loved you...yes. As I thought you loved and wanted me. Are you telling me that that's completely gone?"

Rafe..."love"..."want"... Tanya could hardly believe what she was hearing. But it was in his eyes. At least the wanting was.

Her mind seemed to burst into a mad jangle of needs and desires that had no relationship to any common sense. Oh, why, why, why couldn't she hold on to some common sense when Rafe looked at her like this? She knew what he would do to her if she went back to him. Men never changed. As Grandma said, not even over thousands of years. So why was she so foolish as to still want him...and love him?

She was vaguely conscious that she could barely breathe, that her body was surging with waves of heat, that her lips were quivering. Her hands rose, instinctively reaching out...appeal, want, hope...

She saw some inner anguish twist across his face. Then he was moving towards her...fast urgent strides...reaching for her...crushing her to him...his body shuddering relief at her boneless submission.

"I want you, Tanya. I'll always want you," he rasped, burying his face in her hair, pouring feverish kisses through it, rubbing his cheeks, his chin, his lips, against its fine silky texture. She felt it cling to him, crackling with a live electricity, firing a rapturous excitement of the senses, a stinging desire that swept over

her skin, raced through her nerves, arousing sweet
havoc through her whole body.

Her arms slipped around his waist, under his suit
jacket, locking the hard contours of his body into
more intimate contact with her own yielding softness.
She wanted the feel of him, wanted the taste of him,
the scent of him, the sight and sound...all of him
forever and ever.

"Tanya..." A deep groan of need.

A hand curved around her buttocks, half-lifting her
to meet the questing surge of his arousal. His other
hand slid up her back to clutch a fistful of silky tresses,
wind it through his fingers, gently tug her head back.
He kissed her eyes, her nose, her mouth, nuzzled the
corners of her lips, flicked his tongue sensually inside
them, tantalizing, darting movements, infinitely seductive.

He was so good, so knowingly good. His skin was
soft and smooth against hers, the fresh tang of his after-shave sharpening the scent of his aggressive male-
ness. Intoxicating. She moaned his name, and his
tongue played softly across hers as though tasting it,
pausing to drink in the sound of it...sweet, dark,
drowning sensation.

Passion exploding, his kiss deepening, ravishing her
mouth with the mimicked act of possession. And
Tanya didn't want it to stop. She wanted it to go on
and on whirling her into endless sensation. Her nails
sank into his back as the powerful thrust of his body
seemed to coil into her stomach. The heat of him
seemed to penetrate her bones, melting them in exquisite anticipation. She felt him tense, then shudder,
and his mouth withdrew from hers. He made some

thick sound of self-disgust, threw his head back, then gently pressed her face to the strained cords of his throat.

"Tanya..." A hoarse plea. She felt his convulsive swallow. "Come home with me, Tanya."

Dear heaven! She wanted to. Anything to be with him like this. To have and to hold. Her body clenched in yearning for it. Her blood was throbbing at every pulse point. Her skin was alive with sensitivity. Rafe...her husband...the man she loved...her only lover...Rafe.

But after all the passion, what was left? Would he look at his watch, decide there were other things to do that excluded her? That took him to Nikki? Tanya desperately wanted to say, "Yes, Rafe. I'll come with you to the ends of the world." But she had already said that, as had he on their wedding day. And it was only a fantasy. Nothing to do with reality at all!

He kissed away the hair that waved thickly over her ear, licked erotically at the sensitive lobe, murmured into her mind, "You belong to me. You know you do. You're mine, Tanya. We belong together. Come with me now. All night, my darling..."

His possession. Back in the golden cage again. Displayed on his arm. His wife in his bed. But nowhere else. Never anywhere else. Wasn't she worth more than that? her mind cried plaintively. But at least she would have part of him, her heart answered. Even if she had to share him with Niki.

Dear God! Did she have to do that for the rest of her life? Facing that again, day after day, year after year, just to have Rafe in her bed...making love to her...but not loving her. And what of when she grew older and less desirable, and there was nothing else, nothing else at all?

It was so typical. Rafe's answer to every problem in their relationship was to take her to bed and make everything else seem trivial and meaningless beside what he gave her there. But it wasn't trivial. And it wasn't meaningless. Especially when Niki Sandstrom showed her up so badly in comparison.

"No..." It was a raw moan of protest, dredged from the depths of her disillusionment.

"Don't say that!" he instantly rasped, and his hands moved over her, feverishly, knowingly possessive. His mouth sought hers, intent on blotting out any other thought but of what they shared together.

How Tanya found the strength to do it she didn't know. She clamped her mouth shut against any seductive invasion, dragged her hands back to his hips, pushed violently out of his embrace and sheered away from his nearness in almost blind panic, stumbling against an armchair before scrambling around it to put it between them.

"Tanya ... what in hell!"

He looked more ruffled than she had ever seen him, agitation working over his face, blue eyes ablaze with emotion and passion, hands still outstretched to her.

She was trembling so much she could barely stand upright. She clutched the back of the armchair to steady herself. Clutched even more frantically at her self-respect. Her mind jabbed out its jealous poison. It spit off her tongue with vitriolic harshness.

"What's the matter, Rafe? Doesn't your precious personal assistant measure up in bed?"

He looked at her in stunned disbelief. "For God's sake, Tanya! You're my wife!"

Her mocking laughter held a strain of hysteria. "She's your wife, Rafe! Your wife in everything but bed. I'm just a body that satisfies your carnal urges. You share everything important with her. You use me as the desire takes you."

Anger tightened his face. "Niki Sandstrom works for me. That's all!" he said tersely. "You wouldn't imply such things if she were a man."

"If she were a man, she wouldn't hate me as she does," Tanya retorted fiercely. "She wouldn't come between us as she does. She wouldn't put me down as she does. And you wouldn't defend her as you do."

His mouth compressed into a grim line. "This is between us, Tanya. We are not going to drag Niki into it," he bit out furiously.

Tanya's chin came up. Her eyes blazed a bitter challenge. "Fine! Then go on home, Rafe! Alone!"

He threw up his hands in disgust. "You are insanely jealous!"

"I'm not jealous at all! Those are the facts!" she yelled at him.

One of his hands sliced down in a violent scissor movement. "You want to bind me up. To make me your absolute possession."

Tanya laughed incredulously. "How you twist things, Rafe! That's what *you do to me! That's* what *you* want. Not what *I* want at all!"

His eyes glittered with barely suppressed fury. "Everything I have to do away from you ... you want to stop it. Business meetings, Niki Sandstrom, any work projects at all—"

"Which, of course, you share so intimately with her!"

"As I would with anyone who had worked closely at my side for ten years!" he shouted.

"And who puts me down at every opportunity!" she shouted back. "You don't even give me a chance to share what you're doing, because you already share it with her. And she loves me being ignorant of what's really important to you. She loves seeing me made a fool of when people ask me questions about you and I can't answer them. *She* can answer them..."

"It's better if you don't know too much," Rafe broke in curtly.

"You don't trust me to keep my mouth shut, do you?" Tanya spat back. "You think I'm a dim-witted idiot who'll spill all your secret strategy! Well, it so happens I do have a brain, Rafe. And I know how to be discreet. When I worked for Harry Graham—"

"I wondered when you'd bring *him* into this," he jeered.

A burst of adrenaline surged through her veins. Tanya tossed her head high. Her nostrils flared with haughty contempt for his gibe. "You keep Niki Sandstrom, Rafe, and I'm going back to work for Harry Graham. I'll work as closely with him as she does with you."

"No... you... won't!"

"Yes... I... will!"

The air between them shimmered with the violent clash of will. Tanya was fiercely determined not to cave in. And knowing Rafe as she did, she viewed the gradual rearrangement of his expression with darkest suspicion.

Good old Rafe. She could read his reactions so accurately. Control above all else. Facial muscles visibly relaxing. Orders going out from his mind; temper the voice to sweet reason, look at her with soft indulgence, smile an appeal, give her something that will keep her happy for a while.

And so it came to pass.

Bit by bit.

First the smile. Apologetic. "I'm sorry. I know that Graham means no more to you than Niki means to me." Sweet reason. His hands spread out in an appeasing gesture. "But Tanya, there's no need for you to work. And apart from that, I've been thinking that perhaps it was selfish of me to want to wait for a while before starting a family. If you really want to have a baby now, then that's what we'll do. We'll start straightaway."

Her heart lurched. Rafe actually giving in. Letting her have a baby.

It's a bribe, her mind shrieked. A new toy to keep Tanya busy and content and out of his work life. Like the house and the decorating and all the shopping for clothes.

A baby, her heart moaned in yearning.

But life with Niki would go on as before, her mind dictated in rapid counterargument. This was Rafe's bargaining card. The deal. And for him, it had to be an enormous concession, because he had made it painfully clear that he didn't want a family. *Not yet.* Which meant it was enormously important to him that his way of life be retained just as it was. And if the baby kept her very busy, that poisonous blonde would have even more of Rafe.

It hurt to say it. It hurt very badly. But she forced the words out. "No. I don't want your baby anymore, Rafe. Not unless you get rid of Niki Sandstrom."

There was no gradual change of expression this time. It leaped straight to furious frustration. "You are being totally unreasonable," he grated.

Tanya glared back at him, ignoring the pain in her heart, stubbornness taking firm root in her mind. "It's either her or me, Rafe."

"Goddammit, Tanya!" he exploded. "Niki doesn't deserve to be kicked out of a position she's earned, just because you've let your mind fester with stupid—"

"I'm not stupid!" she screeched at him. "And that's precisely the kind of line she feeds you about me. Doesn't she? Doesn't she, Rafe? She looks down her nose at me with that condescending contempt—"

"You only imagine that!" he snapped.

"Like hell I do!" Tanya seethed back at him. "You might be blind about her, but I'm not! And I'm not going to spend the rest of my life with her looking over your shoulder, Rafe. So you make up your mind whom you want most. Because you can't . . . have . . . both of us!"

His eyes flared with fierce pride. "I will not have you forcing me into this kind of business decision, Tanya! I've always made up my own mind."

"You're absolutely free to make up your own mind anytime you like!" she flung back at him, her own eyes glittering with equal ferocity.

The fuse was lit and sizzling towards the final cataclysmic explosion. Whether Bea Wakefield had judged her entrance to a nicety, or whether it was pure coincidence, both Tanya and Rafe were far too immersed in their confrontation to even admit such a wondering thought to their fraught minds. To both of them she was a totally unwelcome distraction as she stepped into the sitting room, bearing a tray of tea things.

Bea looked blandly at the two glowering figures and said in her soothing-troubled-waters voice, "Why don't we all sit down and have a nice cup of tea while we have a good talk?"

Rafe sucked in a deep breath and turned to her, his eyes as cutting as knives. "Bea, you are all I could wish in a mother-in-law. But this is not the time for a cup of tea. Or a friendly chitchat."

"He's right, Grandma," Tanya agreed tersely. "We don't feel civilized enough to drink tea together. Or do anything together while Rafe keeps his other woman."

"She is not my other woman!" Rafe thundered.

Tanya swept towards the door with fiery dignity, then paused to fling down the final gauntlet, her eyes stabbing their challenge at Rafe. "*Her* or *me!* Let me know when you make up your mind."

Then with a toss of her cloud of red hair, she stalked down the hallway into her bedroom and slammed the door, grimly satisfied with the knowledge that Rafe would not kick a door open in this house. Or he would have to answer to Grandma. She didn't think even Rafe was foolish enough to invite that kind of trouble upon himself!

Back in the sitting room, Bea Wakefield eyed Tanya's husband with rueful sympathy. "Now that we're alone, perhaps you would like a cup of tea, Rafe," she offered.

"No!" he snapped, then made an attempt to re-collect himself. "Thank you, but no." He started pacing around the room like a caged tiger, his hands clenching and unclenching, his face working through a violent range of emotions.

Bea set the tray on the low table in front of the television. She poured herself a cup and sat down in her favorite armchair.

"Your granddaughter is totally unreasonable!" he shot at her.

"Possibly," Bea said noncommittally. "I do wish you'd sit down, Rafe. Perhaps you'd like to talk to me about Niki Sandstrom."

"No!" he seethed. "There is nothing to talk about!"

"It has always been my opinion," Bea said musingly, "that there can be worse kinds of infidelity than the merely sexual."

"Bea... this is crazy! This is neurotic imagining at its worst!"

Bea sighed. "Rafe, I'm a simple woman with a very simple outlook on life. I've always found that things work out best if you keep to certain simple rules. Right down the line. And one of the first rules for a successful marriage is loyalty to your partner. Total loyalty."

"Fine!" he snapped. Then in a voice laced with acid sarcasm, he added, "You tell that to your granddaughter! When she's in a listening mood! As it happens, I'm not in a listening mood, either. So if you'll excuse me..."

He pulled himself up from the furious pacing and bowed towards her with studied politeness. "Thank you for your courtesy, Bea. Please don't get up. I feel like doing some door banging myself!''

He stalked out of the room on a black wave of violence. A few seconds later the front door banged. Very hard.

Bea heaved a deep sigh. She hoped Rafe hadn't shaken the hinges loose. It was such a pity that one couldn't put an old head on young shoulders, but perhaps a little thought seeded here and there might take root where it was most needed. Although she didn't believe in interfering in a marriage. That was a very good rule. One of the best. If people would only follow good simple rules, she thought, there would be a lot less unhappiness in this world.

She rose from her chair, turned on the television set, then settled back again. Sooner or later Tanya would come out of her room and they would have dinner. Bea reminded herself to check on the stewing peaches in another ten minutes. Another good rule. Something easy to eat. More substantial food might not sit well on Tanya's churning stomach.

CHAPTER EIGHT

TANYA WAS NOT totally unreasonable. She waited several days, giving Rafe a reasonable amount of time to make his decision and let her know. The weekend passed. Two working days passed, days when he would certainly have seen Niki Sandstrom. Every hour that went by with no word from him added to a slow-burning caldron of resentments. It was, of course, only what she expected. Rafe wouldn't give up his precious Niki for anything.

And it proved what she had thought about his offer to have a baby. Rafe didn't want a baby. It was an open-and-shut case of wanting his cake and eating it, too. He had simply tried putting a bit of icing on her slice to keep her sweet.

Her grandmother kept finding a lot of chores for her to do. Not that Tanya minded. Cleaning all the silver was a good savage job. So was weeding the back garden. The dough for the scones she made was almost pounded and kneaded out of existence. Even scrubbing the laundry walls was quite satisfying.

But enough was enough. She was not about to spend the rest of her life waiting for a man who thought another woman was more important than his wife. On Wednesday morning Tanya telephoned

Harry Graham and asked if his job offer was still open.

"It is," he affirmed, then after a slight pause and with quiet concern added, "if you really want it, Tanya."

"I need it, Harry," she replied, an edge of desperation furring her voice.

"Oh?"

Tanya closed her eyes, remembering all too clearly that Harry had seen Rafe's reaction to the idea of her taking her old job back. She took a deep breath. "I've left Rafe," she said bluntly.

"Ah..." The sound of understanding. Then soft sympathy. "I'm sorry it came to that, Tanya."

"Nothing's going to change, Harry," she said with dull certainty. "I'd like the job. It would help."

"Sure! Come in now if you like. Or tomorrow morning, if that suits you better. Just tell me when you want to start, Tanya. Whatever you say will suit me fine."

Harry's kindness and understanding brought a huge lump to her throat. Tanya had an awful feeling she might break down and weep all over him if she went in to his office today. And that would be dreadfully humiliating. If she was going to be a career woman she needed to be cool, composed and efficient...like Niki Sandstrom. Backbone, as Harry had said.

"Tomorrow, if that's all right with you, Harry," she managed huskily.

"Right. I'll look forward to seeing you in the morning then."

"Thanks, Harry."

She heard him sigh. Then with forced brightness, "Cheer up, my sweet. Life is not over. What we ship-wrecks do is take one day at a time and stick together. Stops the storm from beating us to pulp. I know you won't want to talk, so don't worry about that. I'll load you with so much work you won't have time to think about anything else. I'm going to be a slave driver. Okay?"

It drew a grateful smile from her. "Okay."

"And wear your brightest dress," he commanded, "It will cheer up my day."

Hers too, she realized. "You're a true knight, Harry," she said in wry appreciation. "See you to-morrow, as bright as I can be, and ready to work like a beaver."

HARRY GRAHAM WAS as good as his word.

Tanya felt quite nervous about returning to work after such a long break. It helped when several people at the Epping television studios recognized her and said hello, but it helped even more when she walked into Harry's office and he greeted her with a warm welcoming smile, and a lot of extravagant compliments about how gorgeous she looked in the wheat-gold color she had chosen to wear.

The old staff welcomed her back into the fold, which was also comforting. There was only one new person, the replacement for her, Tanya quickly real-ized, which meant she was now an extra who proba-bly wasn't needed. But no one said that. And Harry immediately dropped a research subject in her lap that would test her to the limits, and told her he needed the information yesterday, but he would grudgingly accept all the answers next Tuesday afternoon. No later.

Tanya applied herself with determined dedication. She found she still had the knack of picking out the important points that Harry would want to use in his show. It gave her back her sense of worth. And a satisfying measure of confidence as well. She was good for something besides pleasuring Rafe in bed and being a show wife. And everyone on Harry's staff treated her like a person whose opinions they didn't mind listening to at all.

There were some questions from them about Rafe. It was quickly obvious that Harry had kept the status of her marriage a private confidence. For which Tanya was grateful. She fended off the questions with the partial truth that she had missed being a working woman. This explanation seemed to be readily accepted, although a couple of the old staff remarked with some surprise that they had expected Tanya to embrace motherhood. Tanya had an all-too-ready reply for the question in their eyes. *Not yet*.

The work did keep thoughts of Rafe at bay, just as Harry had promised it would. Unfortunately, it didn't make the lonely nights any easier. She wished the weekend had never been invented when Saturday came and she faced two long days before she could go back to the office.

Her grandmother remarked that all the light fittings in the house could do with a good wash. Tanya got the ladder from the garden shed and set to work, taking them down, washing them of every speck of dust and grime, putting them back up. It was almost noon by the time she had finished. She returned the ladder to the shed and trudged despondently back into the kitchen, thinking that maybe she could prepare something special for Grandma's lunch. Except it was difficult to have any real interest in food.

"There's something for you on the dining-room table, Tanya," her grandmother called from the hallway at the front of the house.

"Okay, Grandma," Tanya called back, half hoping it was another job that might keep her mind off other things.

It wasn't.

On the table was a cellophane packet containing a sheaf of red roses. Beautiful dark red roses just bursting from bud form and all absolutely perfect. Tanya tried to contain the wild acceleration of her heartbeat as she unpinned the small envelope from the bottom of the cellophane wrapping. It was impossible. Her hands trembled as she took out the card.

It bore no message. There was only one word written on it.

Rafe.

Tanya drew out a chair and sat down, her body shaking, her mind in a fever. Red roses for love...was that what they meant? Had she been wrong about Rafe? Had he changed?

Rafe might have needed time to work out some business situation with Niki Sandstrom before asking for her resignation. But if that was the case, why hadn't he told her his intentions? Or did the roses mean he was coming to tell her what was on his mind today?

Maybe any minute now!

And she was a filthy mess!

Tanya tipped over the chair in her hurry to get moving. A vase for the roses first, she thought frantically. She didn't want Rafe to think she hadn't cared about them. Tanya quickly chose the one best suited to the sitting room and arranged the flowers in it. Having placed it to best advantage on top of the television set, she raced for the bathroom.

She showered and washed her hair. She was driven by a galloping sense of impatience as she wielded the blow-dryer, wishing for once that her hair weren't so long and thick. But Rafe liked it that way. And pleasing him was her first priority. If Rafe had got rid of Niki Sandstrom to please her, there was nothing Tanya wouldn't do to please him.

It took her an hour to feel satisfied with her appearance. She put on her best white jeans—Rafe had thought they looked sexy on her—and a green silk blouse that pulled in and tied at the waist. Rafe had always liked green on her. And the buttons were easy to undo if he... Tanya's blood started heating at that thought. She missed his touch so much.

She was glowing with happy anticipation when she went out to the kitchen to start lunch. Her grandmother was already there, cutting up some salad vegetables. "I'll do that, Grandma," she offered eagerly.

"Almost done. You set the table, dear." Her bright hazel eyes twinkled knowingly. "You look very nice, Tanya."

"The roses were from Rafe," Tanya said with a lighter heart than she had had for a long time.

"I thought they might be," came the dry reply.

But Rafe didn't come. Or call. The afternoon dragged by. The long visitless evening gradually ground Tanya's hopes into dust. She went to bed with a heart as heavy as lead.

Sunday brought another dozen roses from Rafe. But no other word, and no appearance. In the black darkness of her bedroom that night, Tanya decided that she had been an absolute fool to imagine for one moment that Rafe would get rid of his indispensable personal assistant. The message of the roses was quite clear to her now. Rafe wanted her... but only on his terms.

If he thought he could woo her back to that old situation, he was in for a rude shock, Tanya vowed with vehemence. Not all the roses in the world were going to make her overlook that woman's prominence in Rafe's life. Not even a baby could do that. But she cried herself to sleep.

It was a relief to be able to go to work on Monday morning, to bury herself in matters that had no relevance to her life whatsoever. She had certainly made the right decision to take the job Harry had offered her. It was a lifesaver.

When she came home from work that evening, the scent of roses permeated Grandma's house. Another dozen perfect blooms were in a vase in her bedroom. Added to the dozen in the sitting room and the dozen on the dining-room table, it was just too much for Tanya. A red haze of rage swept through her mind. She snatched up the vase from her bedroom and took it out to the kitchen where Grandma was preparing dinner.

"They came this morning," her grandmother said.

"I figured that, Grandma," Tanya said, sweeping the blooms from the vase and ramming them into the rubbish bin.

She collected the vases from the sitting room and the dining room and crammed their contents into the rubbish bin as well. Then she fastened the lid on the bin and carried it out the back door and set it near the garden shed, out of smelling range.

"I do need that bin in here, Tanya," her grandmother gently chided when she returned to the kitchen.

"I'll take any rubbish out, Grandma," Tanya assured her.

"They were very nice roses, dear."

"Sending any kind of flowers here is like sending coals to Newcastle. Totally superfluous!" Tanya declared.

"Perhaps they were a gesture," came the mild comment. "I don't really think Rafe thought you needed flowers, dear."

"You're absolutely right, Grandma. I'm sure he didn't think that at all," Tanya retorted tartly. "Rafe doesn't give a damn about what I need."

Her grandmother checked the casserole in the oven, then without even looking at Tanya, asked in a curious tone of voice, "Do you care about Rafe's needs, Tanya?"

"Grandma, I've always done what Rafe wanted!" she replied heatedly. Then in a darker tone, "Until now!"

"Wants and needs are sometimes different," her grandmother said thoughtfully, then shrugged off the subject and went on with preparing dinner.

Tanya brooded over those words. Grandma certainly had it right. Rafe wanted her. But he needed his confidential off-sider. At least, he thought he needed her. That was because he didn't want to change anything that was nice and easy for him! Forget about how it affected his wife! Forget about how that poisonous woman treated Tanya! That wasn't at all important!

Thank heaven—or Harry—that she had a job to go to, Tanya thought as she closed the front door of Grandma's house behind her the next morning. She hurried across the porch to the front steps, then came to a dead halt as she glanced down the street and saw Rafe, lounging against the side of his red Aston Martin.

Her mind blanked out. Her heart stopped, then pumped madly to some totally irregular rhythm. Her eyes drank in every detail of him as though he were a mirage that might suddenly disappear. Her memory prompted the thought that when Rafe looked languid, he was at his most dangerous. It put some stiffening into Tanya's backbone and gave her the will to flout the effect he had on her.

She held her head high and directed her legs to move down the steps. She was extremely conscious of him watching her and a fiercely primitive wantonness fired her blood. *Yes, Rafe,* she thought, *take a good eyeful of what you're missing.* She deliberately rolled her hips, deliciously conscious of her body moving under her clothes; the sensual brush of silk stockings against her thighs, the slight jiggle of her breasts under the light fabric of her amber dress, the foaming of her hair around her throat and shoulders.

Rafe straightened up, his body taut and aggressively masculine as he stepped over to the gate and opened it for her. Her eyes taunted the tight reserve in his as she stepped past him. She had no idea what he was doing here, this early in the morning, but she had no doubt he would soon enlighten her.

"Thank you, Rafe," she said, as he closed the gate after her. "Sorry I can't stop to chat. It would make me late for work."

"I'll drive you," he said, not showing the slightest trace of surprise at what should have been news to him.

Tanya swiftly swallowed her own surprise. His arrogant assumption that she would fall in with his wishes fired the swollen bank of resentments that had simmered for days. "I'd prefer to catch the bus, Rafe. I don't want to take you out of your way," she said airily.

"I've come out of my way to take you, Tanya," he replied flatly, his vivid blue eyes boring steadily through the challenging mockery in hers.

"Have you also gone out of your way to get Niki Sandström out of your life, Rafe?" she asked.

His mouth compressed into a thin line. "I will not be pushed. Not by you or anyone," he bit out.

Which meant no. "Neither will I, Rafe," she retorted, then swung on her heel and headed for the stop, which was two blocks away.

"Tanya!"

It was a call of fierce frustration that she stubbornly ignored. She wished she had kept the rose petals to hurl in his face. Somehow he had learned she was working for Harry Graham again and he wanted to stop it. That was why he had come. His neatly ordered world was falling awry. Control shot to pieces. And it served him right, Tanya thought furiously. He could give his damned roses to Niki if she was more important than his wife!

She heard the Aston Martin's powerful engine thrum into life and sent Rafe a mental arrow. *Go! I don't care! I'm as much my own person as you are!*

But he didn't go. The red sports car rolled up beside her with an insistent toot of its horn. Tanya ignored it, proudly striding on without so much as a glance at it. The Aston Martin kept pace with her, the horn demanding her attention. People in the street turned around to look, curiosity drawn by the commotion. Tanya kept walking. Rafe kept the car and the horn going beside her.

Finally, curiosity got the better of her. It was so totally unlike Rafe to make an exhibition of himself. Tanya stopped and turned toward the car. The car stopped. The hooting stopped. The passenger window opened. She stepped over to it. Rafe had a grim look of determination on his face.

"What do you think you're doing?" she demanded.

"I want to talk to you," he said.

"We have nothing to talk about."

"*I* have."

Tanya pointedly checked her watch. It wasn't a diamond-studded one like Niki's but it told the time, and it gave Tanya a lot of satisfaction to pay Rafe back for all his timekeeping. "I have to be at the office at nine o'clock," she stated decisively.

"I'll get you there," he said.

Tanya hesitated only a moment longer. She wanted to hear what Rafe had to say. Besides, she had already made her independent stance. She opened the door and got into the car. Rafe waited until she had the seat belt fastened before smoothly moving the Aston Martin off again.

He didn't immediately speak. His attention was apparently fixed on the road, even though they had not yet reached the main artery to Epping and traffic was relatively light. Goaded by his silence, Tanya asked, "How did you know I was working again?"

"It occurred to me yesterday that you might have done...what you said you'd do," he answered slowly, still not looking at her. "So I rang Graham to find out."

"You rang Harry?" Incredulity billowed through her mind. She simply couldn't believe Rafe had done that. His pride would surely have stopped him from letting any other man know that he didn't know what his wife was doing.

"Yes," he answered curtly, as though finding the aftertaste of the fact not at all to his liking.

Tanya could only suppose it had been an unconsidered impulse that he now regretted. "Why didn't you ring me?" she demanded resentfully.

He flashed her a bitterly accusing look. "You don't answer the phone when I ring you, Tanya. And you certainly didn't ring me."

That was true.

"I won't be bought with roses, Rafe," she stated with a fine edge of contempt.

"I wasn't trying to buy you." His mouth compressed again. He took a deep breath. "I was trying to say...won't you please reconsider?"

It hurt him to say those words. The effort, the strain, was clearly etched on his face. Tanya was suddenly, sharply ashamed of the way she had treated him this morning. He *had* come to her. In circumstances he must hate. And he wasn't even fighting her over her job with Harry Graham.

"Have you reconsidered, Rafe?" she asked quietly.

His fingers worked over the steering wheel, gripping and regripping. He did not look at her. "If you mean about Niki...no," he said finally. "I can't feel right about that, Tanya."

And, of course, it was more important for *him* to feel right than for *her* to feel right, Tanya thought. A deep wrenching sadness clutched her heart. She said nothing. There was nothing to say. Rafe's need for Niki Sandstrom made her feel so hopelessly inadequate. She turned her head away and stared blindly out of the side window.

There was a long silence. It was thick with unspoken things. Memories flowed and ebbed through it. Happy memories and painful ones. Eventually Rafe broke it.

"I was wondering..." He paused to clear his throat. His voice had come out very gravelly. "I don't know if it's slipped your mind or not...this Sunday we're expected at my mother's...with the rest of the family...for her birthday celebration."

Sophia's birthday. Tanya had forgotten in the painful turbulence of the past week. It was a big occasion for Sophia, with all her family gathered together to honor her. Tanya remembered last year's party—how much she herself had enjoyed it—how sure she had been of Rafe's love then, before she had understood about Niki.

Tanya liked Sophia. She wished Rafe was more like his mother, so open, so emotional, so giving. She liked all his family and she was going to miss them. "I'll send your mother a gift, Rafe. And write my excuses. Thanks for reminding me," she said regretfully.

There was a short pause, then brusquely, "I want you to come with me, Tanya."

Resentment surged anew. "Take your other woman," she flashed at him.

"Niki is not my wife," he bit out grimly. "I don't want her with me. I want you."

"To put on a show in front of your family," Tanya savagely derided.

He expelled a long breath. "If you want to put it that way...yes. To go without you...to have my family know that my wife has left me...it does make me look...a failure."

Said in a low monotone, and Tanya didn't need to have much sensitivity to know that every word hurt. Again she regretted her quick-tempered retorts, even though they were justified in the circumstances. She didn't want to hurt Rafe. She loved him.

Clearly it meant a great deal to him that his family see him as a success...someone to look up to and draw strength from. Which they did. And it was so unlike Rafe to open up and admit anything personal. Or to confess to any failure in any way whatsoever.

For some reason the words Grandma had spoken to her last night slipped into her mind. "Do you care about Rafe's needs, Tanya?"

Maybe this was a very deep need for Rafe, more meaningful than a matter of pride. After all, he had sunk his pride to ask her to go with him. In the old days, before they were married, she had felt his deep love for his family. For all of them.

Except her.

She swallowed her bitterness. Did it really matter if she was a show wife for him one more time?

"All right, Rafe," she conceded quietly. "I'll go with you to your mother's birthday party."

She heard his breath rush out on a sigh of relief. "Thank you, Tanya."

"What time do you want to set out?" she asked matter-of-factly, determined that he not think he'd won all his own way with her.

"Would ten o'clock be convenient?" he asked.

Tanya felt pleased that he wasn't taking too much for granted. "That will be fine," she agreed.

No more was said until Rafe pulled up at the gateway to the Epping studios. Tanya flashed him a wry smile. "Thanks for the lift."

He responded with the dazzling smile that had always trapped her heart. "My pleasure," he said.

It took all Tanya's strength of will to get out of the car and on her way. She could feel Rafe's eyes burning after her, knew that he watched her until she was out of sight.

She couldn't help wondering if she had made a foolish decision to give in to him over Sunday. It would be so easy to succumb to that smile of his. But she mustn't. Not so long as he held on to Niki Sandstrom. Sunday was only about using her, as he had always used her. Tanya had to keep remembering that.

It was strange that Rafe hadn't argued with her about working for Harry Graham. Was that because the issue of his mother's birthday was so important that he hadn't wanted to antagonize her over anything else? Or was it possible that Rafe was finally making concessions to her needs? After all, he had changed his mind over starting a family.

The question niggled at Tanya all day. Late that afternoon, after she had finished briefing Harry on the research she had done for him, she couldn't resist asking him about Rafe's call.

"He asked me a direct question. I gave him a direct answer," was Harry's noncommittal reply.

She gave him a puzzled look. "I thought you were set on protecting me, Harry."

"Did it do any harm, Tanya?"

"No," she admitted.

He leaned back in his chair, lifted his feet up on his desk, put his hands behind his head and heaved a deep sigh. "From experience, let me tell you something, Tanya. Divorce is not something I can recommend. There's no one I know who's been through it who enjoyed it. I know its pains very intimately."

His soft brown eyes held all that pained knowledge as he continued. "It starts with a breakdown of communication. You start not saying the things you should say to each other. Then it gets to the absurd point where you can't even say the easy things. No talk. No communication. Everything, every little thing, gathers dark undertones, feeds resentments, and you make mountains from them. And the mountains get too high to scale.''

He gave her a rueful little smile. ''Now I don't know what's going on between you and Rafe. It's better if I don't know. But I remember how it was between you two, and I'd be sorry to see you part. Maybe it was you who made the mountains, Tanya. Maybe it was Rafe. Either way, it's better if Rafe knows what's going on. Knowing is better than not knowing. Talking is better than not talking. At least then you have a chance of seeing and accepting the other person's point of view.''

That was true, Tanya thought. She was glad she had got into the car this morning. It really was awful, not knowing what was going on. Imagining things. She suddenly realized how awful it must have been for Rafe the night she hadn't gone home...not knowing...and imagining things. Although it was his fault for wanting to get rid of her and have only his reliable woman at his side.

''Mountains are very lonely places, Tanya,'' Harry said softly. ''When you first sit on one, you think you're in a wonderful place, lord and master of all you survey. The actuality is different. You're alone. Speaking as one who knows.''

She frowned. ''Do you think Rafe is changing his mind?'' she asked uneasily.

Harry shrugged. ''Perhaps he's minding other things a lot more than he once did. It's one hell of a jolt when a woman leaves you, Tanya.''

''It's all of his own doing,'' she said grimly.

Harry sighed and tipped his chair back a bit farther. A world-weary cynicism dragged at his face, making him look every one of his years. His eyelids drooped. The smile that played around his mouth was not really a smile, and when he spoke, his words were gently mocking.

"Oh, it always is, Tanya. It always is...all the other person's doing."

Tanya got the message. In the end, she had to solve her own problems. And if she kept casting stones, she would keep on breaking windows, and nothing would ever be solved.

She was glad now that she had agreed to spend Sunday with Rafe and his family. At least it gave them the opportunity to be together, and the time to reach a better understanding. It was worth the effort to try anyway.

Mountains, she decided, were very cold places. Especially at night.

CHAPTER NINE

TANYA WAS FULL of resolutions on Sunday morning. She was not going to fight with Rafe. She would do her absolute best to have a calm and rational conversation with him while they were traveling to and from Sophia's home. Hopefully, there might be a meeting of minds for once, instead of bodies only. Naturally, while they were with his family, she would act the adoring wife—which wasn't really hard—and perhaps Rafe would be so pleased with her he might listen to her feelings about Niki Sandstrom, instead of dismissing them out of hand.

A divorce was not what Tanya wanted at all.

But there were some things that just had to change if she and Rafe were ever to have a good relationship within their marriage.

Since Sophia would expect everyone to be in their Sunday best, Tanya dressed in a sea-green silk suit, which had cost the earth. But Rafe had insisted she buy it. It certainly projected the wife-of-a-most-successful-man image, so Tanya figured it was the perfect choice.

The style was figure-hugging with a cinched-in waistline and a pencil-slim skirt, although the skirt didn't look pencil-slim on Tanya. It emphasized her voluptuous curves in an extremely eye-catching manner. Tanya wondered if that was the reason Rafe liked the suit so much. He always said she had the sexiest bottom he'd ever seen. Tanya wasn't above reminding him of that today.

She wore black patent shoes with very high heels, and made liberal use of the *Poison* perfume on all her pulse points. Although Tanya did not want her marriage to Rafe based entirely on sex—as it had been— she figured there was no point in letting Rafe forget what was good between them. It might make him pause long enough to give more consideration to other aspects of their relationship.

So when Rafe arrived at Bea Wakefield's house, promptly at ten o'clock, Tanya was all primed to make the most of the day.

It started well.

Rafe looked devastatingly handsome in a charcoal-gray suit, and he looked at Tanya as though he could hardly bear not to eat her up on the spot and forget about everything else. It was a very satisfactory look, well worth all her thought and effort. True to form, however, Rafe had himself under tight restraint in very short order. He did not try to take her in his arms, or kiss her. He complimented her on her appearance and offered his arm to lead her to the car.

Tanya was grateful for the physical contact. Her legs felt like jelly, which made it rather difficult for her to walk elegantly in her very high heels. The muscles in Rafe's forearm were hard and tight. Tanya reflected how strange it was that sexual desire made men tense, while it wrought the absolutely opposite effect in women.

"You needn't have bought my mother a gift, Tanya," Rafe remarked with a nod towards the parcels she held in her hand. "I've taken care of that."

Tanya threw him a chiding look. "I like your mother, Rafe. I wanted to buy her something."

He smiled.

Tanya's heart turned over.

He opened the passenger door of the Aston Martin and she managed to sink gracefully onto the seat and swing her legs in. Her mind was dazed by how much she loved him as he closed the door on her. She watched him stride around the hood to his side, adoring everything about him.

It took several seconds for the smell in the car to tickle her olfactory nerves, a couple more seconds before the message got through to the identification bank in her brain. Rafe had just stepped into the car and closed his door when the answer exploded into Tanya's mind, blowing all her loving thoughts and all her good resolutions into irrecoverable smithereens.

She turned on Rafe, her vivid face alight with passionate intensity, her green eyes burning with jealous fury. "This car reeks of Niki Sandstrom's perfume!"

He grimaced. "I'm sorry, Tanya, I did my best to get rid of it...."

"How dare you come from her to me!" she screeched. "And expect *me* to play out a charade for *your* family!"

She swung from him towards the door, her hands jabbing at the handle.

"Tanya—" hard, urgent "—there is an explanation."

"I won't do it!" The door handle didn't work. "Goddamn you, Rafe! Unlock this door! I'm not going with you! Not anywhere! Not anyplace! Not ever again!"

"I didn't come from Niki to you!" he declared vehemently.

Her eyes flashed bitter scorn at him. "You think I'm stupid? Perfume doesn't linger long anywhere! She's been in this car this morning, you...you two-faced bastard! Now let me out of here, or so help me, God, I'll claw your eyes out, Rafe Carlton!"

"Niki has not been in this car this morning!" he thundered. "She spilled a bottle of perfume." He grimaced in vexation. "I thought I'd washed the smell out."

"And when did you do the washing, Rafe?" Tanya hurled at him, her teeth bared for a stab to the jugular. "Since last night?"

"It doesn't matter!" he snapped, but a bright slash of red colored his cheekbones.

"Since...last...night?" Tanya bit out, her eyes not giving one inch in the accusation.

Rafe thumped the steering wheel in frustration. "All right! Since last night! I took her out to dinner."

"Another one of your business dinners, Rafe?" she demanded scathingly.

"Yes. No. Yes," he answered, shaking his head in anguished dilemma.

"That's about as ambivalent as your relationship is with that woman. Business...and personal," Tanya drawled meaningly.

He turned blazing blue eyes on her. "Dammit, Tanya! It's not what you think!"

"Yes, it is!"

"You know it's not! I'm sick to death of you bringing her up all the time!"

"And I'm sick to death of you sharing more with her than you do with me!" she retorted fiercely. "I'm good for bed, good for show, but she's better for everything else. Isn't that the fact, Rafe? And that's why you're hanging on to her...."

"She is not the cause of our problems!" he shouted, then made a supreme effort to bring himself under control again. The blue eyes stabbed bitter accusation at Tanya. "Even if I got rid of her, it would change nothing between us," he said in a slowly punched death sentence to all of Tanya's hopes.

A black cloud of despair rolled through her mind. "Oh God, Rafe!" she choked out. "You don't know what you have just said." A doll-wife, that was what he wanted. Nothing more. Ever.

A look of disgust crossed his face. "If you must know, nothing happened between Niki and me last night." He spoke in the overpatient tone of someone talking to a backward child. "Nothing is going to happen. The truth is...we were talking about you. I—" he sighed and grimaced again "—needed some advice."

A blaze of rage slashed into her despair—red on black. "Oh, lovely!" Tanya declared at her sarcastic best. "I'm sure she was very understanding when you told her what a bitch I am! She would have been so sweet and sympathetic. Lightness and brightness at its best..."

"As a matter of fact, she was!" he sliced back furiously. "She would do anything to help me... us. Even to offering her resignation!"

"Which, of course, you refused!"

He dragged in a deep breath and slowly expelled it. "The decision was left in abeyance."

"Pending further developments? Like whether you can get Tanya back into her sex-doll role again, and still keep your reliable woman at your side for the important things," Tanya shot at him with towering sarcasm.

"Tanya..." he grated through clenched teeth. "Because of your jealousy, and for my sake, Niki Sandstrom offered to give up a career position that she has worked ten years for. Just so I can get my wife back—who happens to be so damned selfish she can't think of anyone but herself!"

"And that's why I'm in this car, isn't it? Because I'm so damned selfish I didn't want you to look like a failure in front of your family," Tanya hurled at him. "And while I'm trying to please you, you're out with Niki Sandstrom pouring out all of our private life. Nothing's sacred from her. Not even what you feel about me. She knows it all, doesn't she? She knows more about what you feel about me than I do. Because you tell *her*, and you don't tell *me!*"

He frowned. Tanya had the grim satisfaction of seeing a look of guilt flicker over his face. At least she hoped it was guilt. It damned well ought to be guilt! But it was short-lived.

"And just how much of our private life has remained sacred from Harry Graham?" Rafe quietly retorted, his eyes glaring his suspicion.

"The only thing Harry knows about us is that we're apart," Tanya said forcibly, frustration welling up again over his blindness.

Why were men so easily deceived about relationships? Rafe might be one of the world's great deal makers, but he was a total babe in the woods when it came to dealing with the personal feelings of women. He just didn't understand.

And, if he thought he could justify his infidelity with a counteraccusation, he could think again. She would fight him to the death on that!

Maybe he saw the bitter resolve in her eyes, or he privately acknowledged he had no grounds for his suspicion. Whatever the reason, his expression changed, became hard and grim. There was a dark hungry look in his eyes as he said, "I want you, Tanya. Want you very much."

"I know that, Rafe." It was why he'd married her, why he still wanted to be married to her.

"I'd do just about anything to get you back," he said, obviously hating the necessity, but unable to deny the depth of his desire.

"Wanting is not enough, Rafe," Tanya stated with bitter determination. "There has to be understanding."

Angry frustration contorted his face, but he kept his mouth clamped shut. He slumped back in his seat, closed his eyes and rubbed a hand over his forehead. He heaved a deep shuddering sigh, dropped his hand, then slowly rolled his head towards her. The angry color had left his face. His skin looked drawn and almost sallow. The bleak look in his eyes turned them to a winter blue.

"I don't want it to be like this between us, Tanya," he said in a low weary voice.

All her outrage drained away, leaving her feeling limp and lifeless. "Neither do I," she said dully. "I've tried to tell you. You won't listen. Or you don't want to see." She shook her head in miserable defeat. "Unlock the door, Rafe. Let me get out."

"No...no." He turned his gaze away from her and stared fixedly ahead. His hands rose to the steering wheel and worked agitatedly around it. "I don't know where we're going, but I'd rather us be together," he said slowly. Then he leaned forward, started the engine and drove off down the street.

It was about an hour's drive to Sophia's home. She had kept five acres of the old farm on the outskirts of the city, the section on which the farmhouse stood. She hadn't wanted to leave it, firmly declining Rafe's offer to build or buy her a house anywhere she fancied. She had roots here, she insisted. And good memories. But she allowed Rafe to renovate the house and make it as nice and as comfortable as possible without losing what Sophia wanted to keep.

Neither Tanya nor Rafe spoke for most of the way. Tanya kept thinking about what Harry had said about not communicating. But how could one communicate when one party kept a barrier firmly in place? Niki Sandstrom had eight years' seniority on Tanya, where Rafe was concerned, and she obviously had his absolute trust. How did one fight that? It was a mountain. And Tanya couldn't shift it. All she could do was chip at it.

Maybe she could eventually show Rafe what his oh-so-confidential assistant was really like. If she didn't try, then there was nothing left but ashes anyway. She took a deep breath. Keep calm and poised, she told herself. Don't let anything upset you.

"You told Niki that you were taking me to your mother's today, didn't you, Rafe?"

"Tanya . . . do we have to start that again?" he said with weary distaste.

"Please . . . just answer me," Tanya appealed in a desperate little voice.

"Yes, I told her," came the flat reply.

"Don't you understand how a woman's mind works, Rafe? You can be so clever, and yet so blind."

He shook his head. "What on earth are you talking about?"

"Niki spilled the perfume so I'd know you'd been with her."

"Tanya . . ." It was a pained protest.

"She hates me, Rafe," Tanya said with quiet force. "She hates me because you married me instead of her. Very few women spill perfume. They're always careful of it because it costs so much. Niki Sandstrom would be the last woman in the world to spill anything. She's so very precise about everything she does. I bet you've never known her spill anything before in all the ten years you've been together."

There was a long pause, then in dry gentle mockery, "That doesn't prove anything, Tanya."

"I know how she thinks, Rafe," Tanya persisted. "I know exactly how she would have couched her offer to resign. She could have been one of the world's great actresses. She's so subtle, so clever and so very patient. No wonder you appreciate her role as a deal maker! She can—"

"Tanya," he cut in impatiently, then flatly stated, "Niki was quite genuine."

"Of course it had to seem that way to you," Tanya persisted, keeping her voice very calm. "It was quite a masterstroke on her part, appearing to be so self-sacrificing. But I bet she made her offer in such a way that it made you feel like a fool to even consider losing her, and an even greater fool for giving in to a silly little fool like me who hasn't brains enough to appreciate the bigger picture. She wouldn't use those words, of course. But the implications would be there, gently pressed with deep regret. With all the implications to herself and your business gracefully understated, but nonetheless, implied."

Rafe made no comment. It was clear, though, from the incredulity and surprise on his face that Tanya had guessed right. She held her tongue, wanting her implications to sink in and have some fruitful effect on Rafe. However, further contemplation brought the tight grimness back to his face. Finally he spoke.

"What you're saying... Are you suggesting that Niki Sandstrom is in love with me?"

Tanya took time to think about the question. She knew the answer, but this question was so crucial that she didn't want Rafe to think her answer was some spontaneous outburst.

"Yes, Rafe," she said softly. "In her own unique way, I think she is in love with you. I know she tries to keep you with her and shut me out as much as she can... with very cool, very deliberate, very subtle calculation."

There, it was said. Something Harry hadn't told her about communicating was that it hurt. It hurt badly.

There was a long pause before Rafe responded to her communication, which made it hurt even worse.

"That doesn't make sense," he bit out sharply. "If she were in love with me, which I don't think is the case for one minute, she would have left the day we were married."

Tanya gave a soft little laugh. "Would that have got you out of my clutches and back to her, Rafe? You really think Niki Sandstrom would walk away from something she'd been working towards for more than eight long years?"

His mouth compressed. No reply.

"She rationalized me away as a sexual aberration on your part, and dug in for a long campaign," Tanya went on, deciding she had nothing to lose now. "You never see the wintry contempt in her eyes for me. Or the naked hatred. She's very careful about that in front of you. She wants you to think I'm neurotic. That I'm imagining things. She wants me out of your life so you'll be all hers again. And you're letting her succeed, Rafe. Every day that you hang on to her instead of choosing me, is another feather in her cap."

A longer silence. Her words had obviously set off some internal struggle. Tanya decided it was best to let it run its course. Besides, if Rafe couldn't bring himself to believe what she'd said, saying any more wasn't going to help.

"I think you've got this wrong, Tanya," Rafe said at last. "Niki Sandstrom wouldn't go to bed with me, even if I asked her. Which I have no intention of doing," he added hastily.

"Don't try it, Rafe," Tanya said grimly.

"I wouldn't even dream of it. Niki is a friend."

"She's not a friend to me, Rafe. Or to you, if you value our marriage." She paused, then added with dry self-mockery, "But I guess I'm more easily replaceable."

He gave an anguished jerk of his head but kept his mouth clamped shut. There was no time for more talk anyway. They had reached their destination.

Show time!

CHAPTER TEN

RAFE TURNED the Aston Martin through the gateway to Sophia's property and drove slowly up to the house. There were already several cars lined up under the old coral trees that provided shade from the midday heat. Tanya realized that Rafe had not been driving at his usual efficient speed and they were later arriving than he had intended to be. Punctuality shot to pieces by too much else on their minds.

He parked the car beside the others and quickly alighted, striding around to open Tanya's door for her. Rafe was always meticulously courteous. And, of course, they both had to put a show on for his family. Tanya tried to block out the despair that weighed so heavily on her heart. If this was her farewell performance, she would go out on the best note she could produce.

Rafe opened her door. He lightly grasped her elbow to help her out of the low-slung seat. Then to Tanya's startled surprise, he drew her into a gentle embrace. Her eyes flew up to his, hopefully searching for the love she desperately wanted from him.

The dark unhappiness that looked back at her found its echo in her own tortured heart. He lifted his hand to her cheek in a tender caress, perhaps a need just to touch. "You're not replaceable, Tanya," he said thickly.

What made her do it she didn't know. Instinct? Her own deep clawing need? "Neither are you, Rafe," she whispered huskily, then turned her face to press her lips to his palm in a soft aching kiss.

His breath hissed out in a yearning rush. His hand streaked through her hair. He moved, curving her body to his as his mouth came down on hers, sending her head back against his supporting hand with the force of his passion. Her lips parted willingly to the urgent demand of his, and once again Rafe swept her into a wild current of desire, igniting all her senses with the vibrant reality of her need for him.

There was a terrible hunger in his kiss, a hunger that drew relentlessly on all she would give him, and Tanya couldn't fight him over this. She wanted him too much. Loved him too much. The kiss went on and on, as though he could never have enough of her, and Tanya reveled in the fire that raced through her veins, knowing that it raced through his, too. They were both sinking fast into oblivion, losing themselves in each other, totally heedless of where they were or what they were supposed to be doing.

"So! This is why you are late!" Sophia's rich contralto voice broke into a delighted laugh. "You are just like your papa, Rafe. You cannot keep your hands off your wife!"

Rafe broke away from Tanya, retaining only an arm around her shoulders as he turned to his mother. His face was darkly flushed. "I am sorry, Mamma..."

Sophia laughed away his apology. "It is good that you love each other so much," she declared, giving him a big hug and kissing him on both cheeks. Then she beamed maternal approval on Rafe's wife, took Tanya's hands in hers and pressed them in affection-ate confidence. "I used to have a figure like yours, Tanya. Ah, it did excite the men, particularly Rafe's papa. That caused all the children and I got a little plump."

Which was an understatement. Sophia was a lot plump. Nevertheless, despite the amplitude of her curves, she was a fine figure of a woman, who carried herself with enormous dignity. With her flashing dark eyes and the rather heavy sensuality of her features, she was still not past drawing glances from men, but after Papa—as she always called Rafe's father—she was not interested in taking another husband.

To Sophia, her Australian husband had been a man among men. So strong, so virile, and with hair the color of gold, eyes so blue...irreplaceable. After him, another man could only be a bitter disappointment.

"Mamma, you look more beautiful with every passing year," Rafe said smoothly, giving his mother the admiration that made her glow with pleasure.

"Rafe, you are getting to be a bigger and bigger liar every year," Sophia demurred laughingly, although the compliment had delighted her. "But I'm your mamma, so I forgive you."

Tanya looked at the two of them. A world apart, she thought, and yet so close. Sophia, so open, her feel-ings so instantly displayed—on her face—her voice—her expression. Rafe, sealed up as tight as a pha-raoh's tomb.

"Papa was a passionate lover," Sophia declared with open pride. "Ah, those were the days! I was young and attractive then, wasn't I, Rafe? Not like now. Sometimes, before I could get the little ones off to bed—'' her eyes twinkled at Tanya in happy memory. "Papa, he could not wait. And Rafe was so good at taking care of the little ones. He would always bathe them and put them to bed."

"Yes," said Rafe dryly. "I had a lot of practice at it."

Sophia rippled with laughter. She kissed Tanya on both cheeks and knowingly whispered, "Rafe will make a very good father."

Except he'd probably had enough of being a father when he should have been allowed to be a little boy, Tanya thought with a sudden stab of understanding. But what was done was done, and she couldn't undo it.

Rafe lifted the gifts out of the car and piled them into Sophia's arms, "Happy Birthday, Mamma," he said with his dazzling smile, successfully distracting his mother from pursuing memories he obviously didn't care for.

Not that Sophia realized that. Her pleasure in Rafe and in his gifts was totally unmarked by any thread of concern for him, or awareness of his feelings. To Sophia, Rafe was in control of his world in a way that she had never been in control of her own.

Tanya began to wonder if Sophia understood much about her eldest son at all. She loved him. Adored him. But Tanya was suddenly quite certain that Sophia didn't really know him. He was simply her wonderful son who could do anything, and did.

In fact, Tanya doubted that Sophia had ever paused to consider that her wonderful son might have needs of his own, which he had kept to himself because he knew they wouldn't be answered. He had been loaded with responsibility from an early age, and he had carried the load because the people who should have—his mother and father—had passed it on to him, and he knew if he didn't carry it, no one else would.

Tanya felt her mind bursting with bright clarity, new insights that seemed to answer so much of what she hadn't understood before. Had Rafe automatically placed her in a Sophia role because he felt such a strong desire for her? Was this why control was so important to him; not to let desire rule his life and seduce him into forgetting his responsibilities? Was it his past she was fighting, and not Niki Sandstrom at all?

No! It was both! She was still fighting that poisonous woman, all right. There was no difference there. But even if he got rid of her, as Rafe himself had said, there was still a problem. Although Rafe had probably not related it to himself.

Throughout the boisterous and freely emotional day-long party for Sophia's birthday, Tanya had plenty of opportunity to observe Rafe's family and his relationship with them. His brothers and sisters came to him for advice, expecting their big brother to have all the answers for everything. Any little problem at all, Rafe would know how to approach it, fix it, alter it. Not one of them thought Rafe might have problems that they might help with.

The plain truth, of course, was that there was little any of them could do for Rafe. He stood alone. But they could have tried understanding him. They could have tried asking if there was anything they could do for him. It didn't enter their minds that Rafe had needs, too. Invincible Rafe. Except he wasn't invincible. No one was.

"Do you care about Rafe's needs, Tanya?"

Yes, I do, Grandma, Tanya silently answered.

She did her absolute best—all day—to answer Rafe's need for his family to believe there was nothing wrong with their marriage. Not only that, but she demonstrated over and over again that Rafe had the most loving attentive wife that any man could ever hope to have.

Her reward was the relief in his eyes, the flashes of gratitude, the heartwarming pleasure in having *her* at his side. Whether it was for show or not didn't matter. She made him feel good. Because she cared, and she showed she cared in a thousand little ways...from seeing that he always had a fresh drink to simply curling her hand around his.

They were the last to leave...of those who were leaving. Rafe seemed reluctant to put an end to the day, and Tanya hoped it was because he didn't want an end to come to this trouble-free time in their troubled marriage. He wanted it to go on and on—just like this—but the reality was that this was only a special day.

Nothing had been resolved, Tanya mused, and then suddenly realized that wasn't true. She had had an important insight into Rafe's point of view...why he didn't want to appear a failure, why he had to be indomitable. It wasn't just for himself. For him to appear anything less would have a shattering effect on others. The day would have been disastrous for all of his family if she had not been with Rafe.

Sophia accompanied them to the car, hinting very broadly that she hoped they would have "good news" for her next time she saw them. It got to the embarrassing point where Rafe felt constrained to say, "Mamma, I waited a long time to find Tanya. We will not be having a family until we both feel ready for it. Please don't press. When we decide . . . we'll let you know."

Sophia hugged Tanya's shoulders good-naturedly. Her adored son would, of course, go his own way. She turned her expressive eyes to Tanya, as if to say, "Men really don't understand. You will have to teach him, Tanya." Except Tanya didn't think she had much chance of teaching Rafe anything.

"Ring me if anything happens," Sophia added by way of stimulus.

"I'll do that, Mamma," Rafe said noncommittally, but Tanya could see the chagrin on his face. Rafe hated being pushed. This kind of talk would only harden his resolve not to have a family.

He settled Tanya into the car before kissing his mother goodbye. Tanya fiercely wished Sophia had not brought up the subject of having a baby. Rafe seemed to sink into a brooding silence as they drove off.

There was no doubt in Tanya's mind that Rafe wasn't ready to have another family. He might never be ready. In fact, it was certainly a measure of how much he wanted to keep her as his wife that he had offered her the baby she wanted. But he didn't really want a baby. *Not yet*, anyway.

They had barely gone beyond sight of the farm-house when Rafe pulled the car over to the side of the road and brought it to a halt.

Tanya looked at him questioningly, unsure what the action might mean. Rafe turned his face to her. There was a different, vulnerable look in his eyes. He reached over and gently laced his fingers through hers, the brown of his skin alternating with her white—strength with softness—interlocking.

"Thank you, Tanya," he said in a raw husky voice, and she knew he was thanking her for more than a superficial performance.

"My pleasure," she answered softly.

His gaze dropped to their interlocked hands. He took a deep breath and spoke without looking up. "Perhaps I have never said...how much it means to me...to have you. And not just for physical pleasure." He shook his head. "I've felt...in lots of ways...that you were my reward." He grimaced. "Don't ask me what for."

Tanya didn't have to ask. She knew. Enough to understand what he meant. Again Grandma's words tripped through her mind..."wants and needs are sometimes different." Tanya was beginning to appreciate that.

Rafe lifted apologetic eyes to hers. "It didn't occur to me that I was being selfish. But I realize now that I have been. I expected you to want what I wanted. I was angry with you when you didn't. I thought I knew all the answers, and that you should fall into step with me. I was wrong, wasn't I?"

Tanya's heart leaped in hope. "Yes, Rafe. You were wrong," she stated quietly, instinctively knowing that humility sat very uneasily on Rafe. She would not back off from what needed to be said, but she was very aware that if she pushed too far, he would close up again.

The blue eyes hardened momentarily. To be wrong was almost a challenge in itself. Then his hand squeezed hers. "I don't want to hurt you, Tanya," he went on softly. "I've never wanted to hurt you. I guess there are a few things I need to sort out."

She nodded, deeply relieved. Things were changing, and changing for the better.

He leaned towards her, an earnest expression on his face. "Why did you leave me, Tanya? Tell me the truth. The real truth. Was it just because of Niki?"

Tanya paused to compose her reply. It was so important to say precisely what she felt. So that Rafe would know. It was not knowing that made everything worse. Harry had been right about that.

"If you had treated me differently," she said huskily, her eyes pleading for his understanding, "as a person rather than a thing, the problem with Niki Sandstrom would never have grown to the proportions it has. She shuts me out, but that wouldn't be so bad if you didn't shut me out too, Rafe."

"I see," he murmured, and moved away, withdrawing into himself, reflecting on what she had just said. "And that's still a problem to you now?" he asked.

Her eyes mocked his wish to dismiss it. "What do you think, Rafe?"

He sighed. "It's still a problem."

She wanted to ask what he was going to do, but knew it was better to restrain herself and not pry. Rafe was opening up to her, but he was still very much the self-contained, self-made man who was what he was. The mold had been formed over thirty-four years. Even cracking it a little was a major operation. She had used a bludgeon in leaving him, but bludgeoning would not get her any farther now. She had laid everything out on the table. It was up to him to choose his future course.

Although he was not promising anything about Niki, she felt there was some hope there. Maybe the blinkers would fall off his eyes if he meant to seriously reappraise the whole situation.

He suddenly smiled, the intimately knowing smile that put goose bumps on her skin and made Tanya intensely aware of herself as a *woman*.

"It really is a catch-22 situation," he said with appealing whimsy. "I'm feeling very deprived. Really deprived. Yet if I ravish you, you'll say I only want your body. If I don't ravish you, we'll both be missing out on what we do best together."

He cocked an eyebrow at her in hope. His eyes simmered wickedly with all the promises of how he could pleasure her. "This may not be the most appropriate place in the world, but do you feel like being ravished, right here, right now, instantly, and without hope of redemption?"

The temptation raced through her like wildfire. She did feel like being ravished, right here, right now. With Rafe that was always an exciting idea. He could make anything unbelievably erotic. The pleasure of the moment would be intense, she knew, but afterwards... when he turned away from her, having had what he wanted...

"No, Rafe," she forced out.

But he saw, he knew what she felt, and the sexual tension that screamed between them belied any rejection of him. "Come home with me, Tanya," he said softly, making it an invitation to share a far deeper ravishment with him than could ever be achieved in a car.

It almost killed her to say, "No," but she said it, then wrenched her eyes from the smoldering promises in his and turned her face to the side window.

She heard his deep sigh. "I thought...from the way you acted today...you might have changed your mind."

"I wasn't acting," she said tautly. "And I haven't changed my mind."

"Tanya..." He made her name a throbbing purr of seduction. He withdrew his fingers from hers, sliding them sensuously over her skin before lifting his hand to her cheek. He tenderly stroked her hair back behind her ear. "Look at me," he murmured.

Her heart crashed painfully around the tight constriction of her chest. Her hands curled into fists of determination, fingernails digging hard into her palms. She wouldn't give in. Never, never, never! If she did, it would be all his way again, and she would be trapped into the role she hated.

She jerked her head around and looked at him, green eyes blazing with tortured wants and needs. "I gave you a choice, Rafe," she bit out grimly. "I meant it. I daresay you could have your way with me now, if you keep pushing it. But it won't make me want to come home with you."

He drew back, frowning, his eyes searching the frenzied resolution in hers. "Today..." He lifted his hands in wordless appeal.

She couldn't bear to keep looking at him. It hurt too much. She stared blindly ahead. "Today was very pleasant, Rafe," she said stiltedly. "Thank you for letting me enjoy it with you. But one enjoyable day does not constitute the basis for a lifetime. You have things to sort out before I'll consider coming back to you."

He settled back in his seat. His deep frustration with the situation swirled around her, squeezing her heart. "I warn you, Tanya," he said grimly. "For you, I will bend so far, but I will not be wound around your little finger to the extent of giving in to what I believe is wrong."

He leaned forward abruptly, fired the powerful engine of the Aston Martin, and shot the car back onto the road. He drove back to Bea Wakefield's house in almost half the time it had taken him to reach Sophia's. Not another word passed his lips. Nor Tanya's. She was biting hers, fighting a well of tears that took a lot of blinking back.

Rafe wanted her to accept that blonde snake in the grass at his side!

He might be more indulgent towards her, not shut her out so much, but he didn't want to get rid of his precious off-sider. He wanted an expedient solution where he kept the best of both worlds. He had decided that she shouldn't feel the way she did... and they were right back to square one. So much for communication! Tanya thought in bitter misery.

Rafe escorted her up to the front porch, neither of them meeting the other's eyes. "Thank you for today," he said gruffly. "I appreciated ... your efforts ... very much."

Tanya couldn't trust herself to speak. She simply nodded. And left him.

CHAPTER ELEVEN

ALL, HOWEVER, was not lost, as Tanya soon discovered. Barely one hour after leaving her on Bea's front porch, Rafe telephoned. When her grandmother asked if she wanted to speak to him, Tanya was only too happy to do so, wildly hoping that this might mean a change of mind from him.

"I'd like to take you out to dinner tomorrow night," Rafe said. "I promise I won't press you for anything else, Tanya. I just want to be with you. Will you accept that?"

"Yes," she said, wondering if it meant any more than what he was prepared to admit at this point. Tomorrow was Monday. He would be seeing Niki Sandstrom. Maybe he had come to a decision after all.

He asked what time would be convenient to her, agreed to her answer and promptly ended the call.

"What do you think it means, Grandma?" she asked, having poured out her earlier despair.

"Perhaps it means that Rafe is not about to give up," Bea answered with a little half smile on her lips.

That became evident as the week unfolded.

Almost every night Rafe asked Tanya to have dinner with him. Not one of these outings was in any way related to business. They were kept absolutely personal. Rafe took her to the best restaurants in Sydney, wining and dining her royally. He asked Tanya about her work for Harry Graham. He told her about the projects he was working on. They conversed on all manner of subjects. He did not touch her, except out of courtesy. He did not even try to kiss her good-night.

In a very controlled and very deliberate campaign to win her back, Rafe was obviously set on proving that Tanya was "a person" to him, and not just "a thing." In one way it was very gratifying that Rafe was trying so hard to please her, but Tanya couldn't help remembering that it had been like this *before* they were married. There was no guarantee it would continue once she agreed to go back to him.

In another way, each meeting was a constant strain from beginning to end. The need to touch throbbed between them, their desire for each other totally unabated, and the enforced lack of any physical expression built an ever-deepening frustration. Tanya knew that Rafe was counting on her breaking.

But Niki Sandstrom remained a fixture in his life.

"Is *she* still with you?" Tanya asked the first evening.

"Niki still *works* for me, yes," Rafe replied with pointed emphasis.

Several nights later, Tanya asked, "Does Niki Sandstrom know you're taking me out like this?"

"I have no idea," he replied dismissively. Then again with pointed emphasis he added, "She does not know it from me."

"You mean you're not discussing our private life with her anymore?" Tanya persisted, caring too much to be left uncertain on this important issue.

Again she thought she saw a flicker of guilt cross his face. Then he looked directly at her, his blue eyes even more vivid with burning determination. "I regret that I ever did. Please believe that, Tanya. And I promise you, it won't ever happen again."

She almost broke then. She desperately wanted to accept all the promises of change that Rafe held out to her. Unfortunately, there was another problem, and each day that passed made it loom larger and bigger, blurring all the other issues.

Tanya had finished the last month's course of contraceptive pills but her period had not come. It had been due the day before Sophia's birthday, although Tanya had not thought about it at the time. Too much else on her mind. It terrified her to think of what might happen to their relationship if she was pregnant. She was absolutely certain that Rafe did not want a baby, yet there was no way in the world that she could contemplate not having it. If there was one.

Tanya let a few more days pass, hoping against hope that her period had simply been delayed because of stress, or something. Finally, with a sense of black fatalism, she forced herself to take a pregnancy test.

It was positive.

The knowledge that she had indeed conceived a child was not the happy knowledge Tanya had once dreamed it would be. Even though Rafe had said— under stress—that they could start a family straightaway, she was all too painfully aware that it was not what he wanted. She well remembered his reaction to his mother's pushing.

Would he believe this conception was an accident, or would he think she had deliberately ignored his wishes and taken matters into her own hands? It had been her decision not to go home that fateful night when she had forgotten all about the pill she should have taken. Rafe would surely blame her for what had happened even when she explained the circumstances.

He might think she had deceived him and would deceive him again if he didn't give in to what she wanted. Any sense of trust might be seriously undermined. Yet it was his child, as well as hers, and Tanya desperately wanted their baby to be born and brought up within the security of marriage.

She knew Rafe wouldn't deny his child that. His sense of responsibility was too strong to deny his child everything it should have. It was the relationship between her and Rafe that worried Tanya. Endlessly.

Yet she could not keep deferring the news forever. She had to make the decision to tell Rafe and follow through on the inevitable course of going back to live with him, even though Niki Sandstrom was still there to make trouble for her whenever she could. At least Rafe had distanced himself from his too-personal assistant in some respects. All Tanya could do was hope it would stay that way so that she and Rafe could work out their problem without that poisonous woman's influence distorting everything.

Tanya was still in the midst of this emotional turmoil when she met Yorgan Yorgansson again. Harry had decided that the Danish entrepreneur would make a good interview on his chat show. Overseas investment interests were a topical and controversial item among Australians who thought too much of their native land was slipping away from them and into the pockets of foreigners.

Yorgansson had come in to the television studios for a preshow discussion on the areas that he was prepared to talk about, and the areas that he declined to comment upon in any way whatsoever. Harry did not aim for confrontation on his show. He aimed for entertainment and well-informed interest, and he liked his guests to be pleasantly relaxed. In line with this aim, he invited Yorgansson to lunch with him, and they were on their way when Tanya inadvertently ran into them in the corridor outside the offices.

Apparently Yorgan Yorgansson's fascination with her was instantly reawakened. He greeted her warmly, discovered she worked as a research assistant for Harry and insisted she accompany them on their business luncheon. Which put Tanya in a considerably awkward position. She didn't want to offend the Dane with an outright rejection if he was doing business with Rafe. On the other hand, she felt uncomfortable with his open admiration of her.

Seeing her consternation, Harry gave her a confidential wink. "Gather your handbag, Tanya. I'll look after you. A little meal will brighten your day."

Yorgan Yorgansson looked a little perplexed by Harry's words, but Tanya was instantly reassured that Harry would protect her from any unwelcome overtures.

They went to a fine restaurant in North Sydney. Harry, as always, was as good as his word, subtly turning the conversation into general areas whenever Yorgan Yorgansson seemed about to pursue anything personal with Tanya. Their entrées were being served when Harry shot Tanya a sharp warning look. Then he smiled and affably remarked, "This must be a popular place for business luncheons today. Rafe has just come in, Tanya."

Her heart rolled over. Here she was with the two men that Rafe was most decidedly suspicious about, and he was certainly not going to like it, however innocent it was. Somehow she forced a surprised smile onto her face and turned to acknowledge him.

Rafe was not alone. Niki Sandstrom was with him. Tanya's forced smile faded. If he could be with her—for work purposes only—she could be with Harry—for work purposes only—and to hell with whatever else Rafe thought! She wasn't guilty of anything.

He had not yet seen her. His indispensable personal assistant was claiming all his attention as they were shown to a table on the other side of the dining room. Then as though he sensed Tanya's eyes on him, he frowned, and darted a look in her direction.

His gaze instantly homed in on her. Tanya constructed another smile and lifted her hand in a hello salute. The blue eyes swept the other faces at her table. Rafe's face visibly tightened before relaxing into a smile as forcibly constructed as Tanya's. Whatever he felt inside, Rafe would never give it away in public. He turned and spoke a few words to Niki, then rose from his chair and headed straight towards Tanya, the smile still in place.

Tanya did have the brief satisfaction of seeing Niki Sandstrom look decidedly vexed with this turn of events, but the cool blonde quickly turned away and concentrated her attention on the menu.

"Hello, darling," Rafe said lightly, then with a polite nod to her table companions. "Yorgan...Graham..." Then back to Tanya. "You didn't tell me you were coming here today." There was not the slightest note of criticism in his voice, merely interested inquiry. But Tanya could feel the inner tension and the thousand question marks in his mind.

"That's because she didn't know," Harry supplied good-humoredly. "I collected her only an hour ago for this business luncheon with Yorgan. Just in case I needed to remember some detail from the conversation. Your wife has an amazing talent for recollecting a conversation almost word-perfectly. Though I'm sure you know that, Rafe. Must be invaluable to you at times."

There was a brief flicker of surprise in his eyes, but he didn't miss a beat. "Yes. I don't know what I'd do without her," he answered smoothly.

Good Sir Harry, Tanya thought gratefully, and was able to smile more openly at her husband. "Don't let me keep you from your business, darling. Your table companion is looking this way. She's waiting for you."

Rafe was unable to conceal his surprise this time. He could not believe that Tanya was taking this so calmly. She could see the doubts forming, shadowing his eyes. Then decision sharpened the blue irises again. "Very well. Have a nice lunch, Tanya. I'll see you tonight. If you still feel like being wined and dined." An edge of sarcasm to it. No gleam of anticipation.

"Yes. I do. I will," she confirmed with a touch of fervor.

A tiny measure of relaxation. "The usual time?"

Tanya realized that Rafe was sending out a message to the other men. Tanya and he might be separated, but she was still his. "Yes," she said, and meant it in every sense. She was his. She might fight him, even hate him for his blindness, and rail against his possessiveness, but when it came right down to the bone, she was his. And she would tell him so tonight. It was stupid to keep dithering.

Rafe smiled grimly at Harry and Yorgan and left them to go back to his own table. Tanya saw her rival's face light up as he joined her. Niki Sandstrom had not given up hope. The only comforting thought was that Rafe didn't want his personal assistant assisting him in bed. At least, Tanya was fairly sure he didn't. Whatever Rafe's thoughts on the matter, Tanya had no doubts in her mind what the all-too-willing blonde would do if Rafe suggested he needed a little soothing for his deprivation. But Tanya would solve that problem tonight as well.

Harry gave a theatrical sigh to draw Tanya's attention back to him. "That husband of yours has always been dynamite to you, hasn't he, Tanya?" he remarked slyly.

"He will always be the only man in my life, Harry," she answered, her eyes dancing her appreciation of his tactics.

With a wonderfully tossed-off utterance, Harry had cleverly stated the situation for Yorgan so that the Dane would give up on his subtle flirtation and concentrate on business.

Yorgan Yorgansson was a pragmatic man who did not pursue the impossible. He shrugged his shoulders. Why were women the way they were? Rafe Carlton was a master deal maker, but he hadn't the faintest idea of how he should be treating Tanya. Why should she love him so?

Imponderable, he decided. He looked at her, found her gut-wrenchingly beautiful. A rare jewel that should always be polished with care. He could have shown her so much, given her anything, but...no hope of success there. Back to business. He turned to concentrate on Harry Graham. A very astute man, Graham. Without the mental force of Rafe Carlton, but very astute.

The rest of the luncheon was without incident. Tanya waved to Rafe as she left the restaurant. He raised his hand in an answering salute. Tanya's eyes flickered over Niki Sandstrom. The blonde head did not turn, not for even the slightest acknowledgment of Rafe's wife. Her ice-cold beauty was focused completely on Rafe. To all intents and purposes, to Niki Sandstrom, Tanya did not exist.

Tanya had to smother an urge to walk straight up and confront her. She knew it would be a no-win situation. She would end up looking like a spiteful cat, and the maligned blonde would retain her cool superior dignity—the injured innocent—earning even more kudos with Rafe.

Tanya decided then and there that in future, she would never accompany Rafe to anything if Niki Sandstrom was also to be there. She might be cutting off her nose to spite her face, but that was something she would never accept again.

When she arrived home that evening, she set about packing her bags. "Things have changed, Grandma. I'm going home with Rafe," she announced.

"Ah! Rafe asked you to come back?" Bea's eyebrows were raised in speculation.

"No. It's a unilateral decision. Same as when I left."

"Well, it's been nice having you, dear, but I'm sure Rafe will appreciate your decision," came the warm reply.

Tanya smiled. Definite approval. However, there was still the problem of telling Rafe about her pregnancy. She hadn't told Grandma about that. Rafe should be the first to hear it. She fiercely hoped he would be so pleased they were together again that he wouldn't mind too much.

There was an exultant song in her heart as she showered and dressed in one of her favorite dresses, a close-fitting sheath in a dramatic fabric of dark red roses on a black background.

When she had finished packing Tanya carried the suitcases out to the front porch ready for Rafe to put them in his car. It was a deliberate signal of her intentions, and she hoped it would make Rafe feel happy that his campaign had succeeded.

He rang the doorbell promptly at seven-thirty. Tanya virtually flung the door open, eager to be in his arms again. The question in his eyes was instantly answered. For one moment he looked at her vividly beautiful face, and then there were several minutes of ecstatic madness. Their embrace fired the passion that had been too long denied. It was so good, so wonderful to be free and uninhibited about...bodies. Their hands moved in urgent touching, mouths met and fused, speaking with all the eloquence of longing and need.

"Do we have to go out to dinner?" Rafe finally asked, his thighs hard and pulsing against hers, his lips still pressing hot kisses through her hair.

"I don't suppose you've been shopping," she answered, reveling in the heady taste of him.

"Some," he breathed on a sigh of intense satisfaction.

They managed, in a somewhat erratic fashion, to take leave of Tanya's grandmother, who looked benevolently amused by their eagerness to be gone.

They bundled the luggage into the car. The air between them crackled with electric anticipation. Rafe drove in a relaxed manner but Tanya could feel his triumph. He had got his wife back. Rafe, the indomitable survivor.

He held her hand except when he needed to change gears. *I hope this is going to work out,* Tanya thought feverishly. *In a day or two, or a week or two, when the novelty wears off, please don't let us return to what we had.* Then the thought of the baby made Tanya realize that there was no retreat to the past. In some ways, everything in the future was going to be different.

She looked at Rafe, and all the pent-up emotion in her heart spilled into words. "I love you."

He squeezed her hand.

Rafe was not good at expressing his feelings in words. Tanya wondered if he thought it a weakness to reveal his innermost emotions. Then she realized that a man like Rafe automatically shied away from showing any vulnerability. But it was there. She had seen it in his eyes several times over the past few weeks. He did feel deeply. He simply kept it all hidden.

They arrived home. Tanya went into the kitchen while Rafe carried her bags up to their bedroom. She wasn't hungry. Food was the last thing on her mind. She opened the refrigerator and stared blindly at the contents on the shelves. Then she felt Rafe's presence and looked up to see him watching her from the kitchen doorway, an expression of satisfaction, contentment and of deep, deep pleasure on his face.

"It's good to see you here, Tanya," he said, and there was certainly a throb of very real emotion in his voice.

She laughed in sheer happiness. "In the kitchen, Rafe?" she teased.

"No." He smiled at her teasing but shook his head. "Here in the house. It's been...very empty...without you."

Which was probably the closest Rafe would come to saying how much she meant to him. He had felt an emptiness that Niki Sandstrom had been unable to fill, Tanya thought with satisfaction.

"What do you want to eat?" she asked.

"I'm not really hungry, Tanya. Whatever you'd like will suit me fine."

Her heart skipped a beat. She knew what he wanted—the hunger was in his eyes—but he was deliberately exercising restraint, considering her needs, considering her feelings. She was a person, not just a body he wanted to possess.

"I'm not hungry, either. Let's skip dinner for a while," she said huskily.

She closed the refrigerator door and walked towards him, her own eyes promising that his deprivation was over, as soon as he wanted it to be. He took her gently in his arms and held her close; just held her as though there was no urgency at all, as though it was enough for him to savor the reality of her close to him. His cheek rubbed over her hair, slowly, tenderly. When he tilted her face to his, he kissed her with a soft sensuality that held no desire at all to rush to passion. Yet to Tanya, it was more moving than any kiss he had ever given her, like a sweet caress on her heart.

Then he lifted his lips from hers and looked down at her face, the blue of his eyes a dark swirl of intense need. "I want to make love to you, Tanya," he murmured huskily. "I want to blot out that last time...and I don't want you to feel again that you're just a thing to me. It's not so, and I want to show you it's not so. Will you let me do that?"

"Yes," she whispered, even more deeply moved by Rafe's desire to make amends for the sins of the past.

He carried her up the stairs, cradling her close to him. Like a baby, Tanya thought, and the question raced through her mind...should she tell Rafe now? Before...or after he made love to her? If she told him before, would he think she had only come back to him because she was having a baby? She did not want to inject any spoiling note into this wonderful moment. Yet if she waited until afterwards, Rafe might think she had been trying to twist him around her finger.

No, no, he couldn't think that, Tanya frantically reasoned. Making love was his idea, and right at this moment it was far more important for Rafe to have his way, to do what he needed to do, and what she needed him to do as well. Their relationship was what mattered most. Then the baby.

He placed her in the middle of the bed and dropped down beside her. His eyes caressed her face as he fanned her hair out on the pillow with gently stroking fingers. "I've missed seeing you here like this, Tanya." His voice was a rough purr. "I've missed the sight of you...the touch...the scent...the taste of you. I've lain awake at night...wanting...aching for you to be beside me...if only to reach out and know you're there...with me."

"I've missed you too, Rafe," she whispered, lifting a hand, sliding it up his shirt, flicking open the buttons so that she could place her palm over the firm warm flesh above the throb of his heart.

A light tremor of pleasure shook him. He gently removed her hand, lifted it to his mouth, pressed a kiss into her palm, then placed it on his shoulder as he leaned down to brush his lips over hers, a kiss that slowly clung and melted all barriers between them.

Tanya happily gave in to Rafe's need to control—this time. Because this time was different. She knew she was not just a body to him. He made love to her with slow exquisite care, arousing her with a gentleness that stirred far more than desire. Tanya felt an overwhelming rush of love for him.

He did not hurry their undressing. He did not hurry anything. The look, the touch of their naked bodies, the scent, the taste...held more fascination, more satisfaction, more pleasure than ever before. The sense of rediscovering what had been briefly but frighteningly lost, lent an extra sharpness to their senses, a deeper appreciation of all they were to each other.

Not even Rafe, with all his mastery of control, could hold back on the wild rhythm of need that enveloped them when her body welcomed the pulsing thrust of his. They hurtled into an abyss that throbbed with dark sweet ecstasy, and when they finally came to rest, they lay entwined, hearts beating as one, togetherness completo.

There was no pulling away, no checking of time. Rafe held her to him as though he could not bear to let her out of his embrace. He kept her hugged to him when he shifted his weight from her and rolled onto his back. His hands caressed ... possessively, but oh, so tenderly. And Tanya was supremely content as she lay with her cheek over his heart, reveling in the sense of having come home ... to where she would always belong ... with Rafe.

Now, she thought, *now I can tell him about the baby. It will be all right. Everything's different now.* She ran her fingers lightly over his hip, and smiled as she felt the little shudder of pleasure ripple under his skin.

"Rafe?"

"Mmm..." He answered her caress with a featherlight glide down her back that made her shiver with pleasure.

"There's something I want to tell you."

"Mmm?" His sensitive fingertips started circling down from her shoulders.

Tanya took a deep breath. "I'm pregnant, Rafe."

His fingers stopped moving. His heart seemed to stop beating. His whole body went unnaturally still. There was no sound from him ... no expression of gladness or joy ... nothing. For what felt like aeons, Tanya waited for some positive reaction from Rafe, but nothing came. The only sign that he was still alive was the almost imperceptible rise and fall of his chest as he kept breathing.

Tanya felt a welling of anger and struggled to suppress it. Hadn't she known all along that he didn't want a baby? Maybe he was struggling to suppress his anger. She rolled away from him and was off the bed and on her feet before he could make a move to stop her, if he had been inclined to stop her. Tanya didn't look back. She didn't want to see what was written on his face...if anything was. What she had wanted to see certainly wasn't there or he would have said something before this.

She strode across the room to her wardrobe, ignoring the shaky weakness in her legs. She opened the door, pulled out her silk wrap, thrust her arms into the loose sleeves, dragged the silk around her nakedness and tied the belt with savage tightness. It helped to calm the trembling a bit.

"I'll leave you to think about it while I search out some food for us," she tossed towards Rafe as she headed for the door to the hallway. Her voice was hard and brittle but she couldn't temper that. She still couldn't look at him, either. She was afraid of losing control, making things worse.

"When did it happen?"

The question was asked in a completely toneless voice. Tanya faltered in her step, halted, took a deep, deep breath. She stood completely still. She knew the value of that stillness now. It was a frozen stillness that covered the darkest deepest waters of life. Control, she thought, and she had to be just as controlled as Rafe or things would be said that might never be forgotten or forgiven. She heard Rafe shift. She turned. He was sitting up. Nothing showed on his face. His eyes were a flat blue.

"Does it matter?" she asked, her voice as toneless as his had been.

"Yes."

She could feel the anger rising...rising. "The night before you raped me," she said, "I missed taking the pill."

She saw shock hit his face, dilate his eyes and felt a savage satisfaction. Then slowly his expression changed, darkening with doubts.

"Niki said you were with Yorgansson two nights later."

It was like a volcano erupting inside her. The frozen stillness cracked. Control broke into jagged shards. Her eyes were fire and ice. "Niki!" she spit.

He had kept Niki Sandstrom despite all she had told him about the poisonous bitch. He had kept her and trusted her and taken her word against his wife.

Tanya trembled with the force of her outrage. She wanted to kill Rafe. Love...hatred...inseparable and consuming everything. Like a sleepwalker she turned and moved towards the bedroom doorway again. She had to get away from him for a while.

"Tanya..."

She kept walking, ignoring the plea in his voice.

"Tanya..." Raw. Urgent.

She heard him move and couldn't bear him to come after her. Not yet. Not until she was capable of sorting this out with some sanity. She half turned from the doorway, her chest heaving from the turbulence inside her, her eyes stabbing him into stillness again.

"This is your child... *your child*..."

She couldn't say any more. A huge lump gorged her throat. Tears blurred her eyes. She blundered along the hallway to the stairs. Maybe it was because she couldn't see properly, or maybe her legs were trembling too much. Somehow she missed her footing at the top of the staircase.

She stumbled, pitched forward, and then the stairs were rushing up at her, hitting her, tipping her down and down, beating at her. She heard Rafe screaming her name, pounding through her ears, echoing, echoing, but the stairs wouldn't let her stop until her head hit something hard and there was black pain... pain fading... into blackness.

CHAPTER TWELVE

RAFE PLUNGED down the stairs—two, three steps at a time—fear clutching his heart, panic and despair and black terror freezing his mind. "Tanya...Tanya..." He heard the hoarse screams tearing from his throat, but she kept falling and he couldn't reach her in time, couldn't stop the rush of her body, the crash of her soft giving flesh on unfeeling wood.

He watched in sickening horror as her head bumped against the newel post. Then came the further heart-wrenching thud as she slumped to the marble tiles of the foyer.

She lay so still, lifelessly sprawled in abandonment of any conscious care. Rafe sank to his knees beside her, his whole body trembling in fear and devastation. Very gently he placed his hand on her neck, feeling for the artery. The slow pulse sent a shudder of relief through him. She was alive. Still alive.

He forced himself to look over her limp body. Very carefully he felt her arms and legs. There didn't appear to be any bones broken. He desperately wanted to gather her up in his arms, hold her close, but he didn't dare move her. If there was any injury to her spine, or her neck, he might do irretrievable damage.

Her face was so pale. He gently stroked the wildly spread tresses of her dark red hair away from it, feverishly willing her eyes to open. She moaned. Moved her head. Her legs curled up. With a groan of intense relief, Rafe gathered her into his arms. Her eyes flicked open, seemed to focus on his face.

"Don't want to lose my baby," she said in a strange floating voice.

"Our baby, Tanya. *Ours,*" he said fiercely. But he wasn't sure she heard him. Her focus had already wavered, seeming to retreat from him. She closed her eyes and sank more heavily in his arms. "Tanya…I'll make certain you don't lose the baby," he cried hoarsely, holding her more tightly, willing her to hear him, to know he would make everything right for her, if she'd just give him the chance.

He waited for what seemed an interminable time, waited for Tanya to come back to him. But she didn't stir again. She lay like a limp doll in his arms, inert, lifeless. He couldn't let this go on. He had to do something. If she died…

Life without Tanya…the thought was unbearable.

His mind went into emergency overdrive. His first thought was to take her somewhere more comfortable. But maybe he shouldn't move her. Maybe carrying her somewhere would be wrong. Doctor first. Ambulance. Get a blanket. Keep her warm.

He followed each step as fast as he could, dragged some clothes on as well. He had to accompany Tanya to the hospital, stand by, be ready to do whatever needed to be done. Having dealt with all he could think of in readiness, he knelt beside her again, holding her hand, barely restraining himself from squeezing it in his need to inject life into her.

She hadn't stirred at all. He found a facecloth and started to wipe her brow, her cheeks, endlessly repeating her name, willing her to wake up. She did not move, and Rafe felt despair eat into his heart. He was deadly afraid...afraid that she might somehow die to punish him for what he had done.

The baby...

Of course it had to be his. Madness to doubt it...to think anything else. Tanya had been right about Niki all along. He had been wrong. So many things he had noticed this past week—the sly double-edged comments—poisonous. At least he had made the right decision about Niki. No more. If only Tanya was all right...

Shame ripped at his heart, bored into his soul. He buried his face in his hands. He didn't deserve to look at Tanya, let alone ever have her again. How could he have let Niki seed that dark suspicion in his mind? What was his life for...without Tanya? Maybe his father had been right all along...it was only the loving that mattered.

He hadn't told Tanya that he loved her...not when she wanted to be told...only when it suited his purpose. She didn't know how much he loved her, how barren his life felt without her. He had been so greedy for her...greedy about everything...wanting it all his own way...

For the first time since he was seven years and two months old, tears came to his eyes. If Tanya lost the baby, he would never forgive himself.

"THE BABY . . ."

"Is safe, Tanya. Everything's fine. The doctor says there's no problem with the baby, darling. Please don't keep worrying."

The words slid into her barely conscious mind . . . Rafe's voice . . . soothing the turbulent blackness into an easier gray. "Safe" . . . the comforting word clung. It felt good. So did the soft stroking on her hand. Warm and caring.

"Tanya . . ."

Rafe was calling her. He sounded as though he was a long way away, but there was a pleading note in his voice and Tanya wanted to respond. She opened her eyes. Things seemed to swim around her but she registered one reality. Rafe right next to her. Not far away at all.

Her focus slowly steadied and cleared. Rafe sitting on a chair, next to her bed—a strange bed—a strange room—and Rafe's face, so drawn-looking, strained, his eyes burning into hers with urgent intensity.

"Where am I?" she asked, struggling to come to grips with the situation.

"You're in hospital, Tanya," Rafe answered, his voice low and soothing again, but she saw the effort it took him, straining his face even more. "Everything's all right. You've got concussion from hitting your head on the stairs, but there's no problem with the baby. All you need to do is rest, and everything will be fine."

Memory stirred. She stared at Rafe as it all came back . . . telling him about the baby . . . the pain of his rejection of it . . . losing her footing on the stairs . . . falling . . .

"How long have I been here?" she asked, fighting the black turbulence that swirled around her mind again.

She saw relief hit Rafe's face. It took him a few seconds to wrench his eyes from hers to glance quickly at his watch. "About twelve hours," he said huskily, his eyes flying back to hers, hope and desperation mingling equally as he searched for a further lucid response from her.

He needed a shave, Tanya thought. His shirt was only half-buttoned. His hair was all awry. Twelve hours... it must be close to ten o'clock in the morning. And Rafe hadn't left her to go to work.

"You've been with me...all the time?" she asked.

He nodded. His fingers—of course, it was Rafe's hand holding hers—worked agitatedly over hers, pressing, wanting more from her.

A wave of deep sadness swept through her as she remembered he had just been reassuring her about the baby...but he didn't want it. He had even thought it might not be his. But he did care about her, Tanya told herself. He wouldn't be here, looking as he did, if he didn't care very deeply.

"I've never been with any man but you, Rafe," she said, her eyes pleading for him to believe her. "I don't want anyone else. Only you."

"Hush..." Sheer anguish twisted across his face. "I love you. No one else." His face expressed the frantic search for words, which came haltingly. "I need you in my life. I need our baby. I need everything that you give me." His voice gathered passionate conviction. "I'll never doubt you again." Then in hoarse pleading, "I've been wrong. I'm so sorry...so terribly sorry."

Tanya stared at him, relief pouring its balm over her inner pain. This wasn't the old Rafe. This was a new man, who hurt and had pains too...and more important...he could tell her. Whatever the scars of his childhood, somehow she had changed them.

"Forgive me," Rafe begged in a voice that shook with emotion.

His need was so explicit it wrenched her heart. Tears blurred her eyes. Rafe...opening up to her at last. "I'll always love you," she whispered, yet in the back of her mind was the chilling figure of Niki Sandstrom, waiting to inject her poison again...to take Rafe away from her.

The tension on his face seemed to dissolve into a wet mist. *Must be the tears in my eyes,* Tanya thought, and tried to blink them away. Rafe muttered something heartfelt but the words were too low for her to hear properly. She thought it was a prayer of some kind.

He lifted her hand to his lips and pressed a long impassioned kiss on her palm. He rubbed her palm against his cheek as though he needed her touch...the feel of her skin, the warmth of her flesh.

She blinked harder. He blinked, too. Then he smiled at her—a pure blissful smile that poured into Tanya, right down to her toes. "I love you," he said. "I always will."

The threat of Niki Sandstrom receded. Rafe was hers. He always would be. Just as she was his.

"I probably shouldn't talk about this," he said softly. His eyes searched hers with wary anxiety as he went on. "I don't want to agitate you, but I know Niki lied, Tanya. You won't have to worry about her. She won't touch our lives anymore. Not in any way. I accepted her resignation yesterday afternoon."

Tanya was totally stunned by this piece of news. "You mean...after I saw you...at the restaurant?"

He nodded grimly. "That was the final straw. The way she ignored you. And what she said about Yorgansson after you left. I didn't want her near me. Ever again. You were right about her. It was hard for me to believe at first. She'd been my right hand for so long in the business that I took her trustworthiness for granted. I'm sorry I didn't realize she was harming us, Tanya. I do now."

"Why didn't you tell me?" Tanya asked. Surely he had known how important it was for her to know that woman was gone.

He grimaced an apology. "I was going to. But then I saw your suitcase on Bea's porch, and when you opened the door, and you'd already made your decision...Niki was blown completely from my mind, Tanya. Having you back again...all I could think of was making sure I did everything right for you...until you told me you were pregnant. And then I..."

He shook his head, a deeply pained look on his face. "I let doubts enter my mind. I'm sorry I hurt you like that, Tanya." The blue eyes earnestly beseeched hers. "That will never happen again. I swear it."

She gave him a rueful little smile. "I'm sorry about the baby. I know you don't want children, Rafe, but—"

"But I do!" he cut in vehemently. "*I'm* not sorry about the baby, Tanya. I want our baby as much as you do. Please don't think anything else."

She stared at him incredulously, yet the blazing sincerity in his eyes assuaged her doubts. "You never wanted me to talk about having a baby," she said tentatively.

He heaved a shuddering sigh and looked ashamed of himself. "That wasn't because I didn't want children, Tanya. I saw what having babies did to my mother. I didn't want that to happen to you. I wanted you to be free. Not to be... always tied down... busy..."

"I understand, Rafe," Tanya broke in softly.

Again his eyes flew to hers, relief showing clearly on his face. "I looked after all my brothers and sisters most of the time. I know how to look after them. So I can help a lot," he said earnestly.

She smiled at his generosity. "I guess being an only child myself... I wanted one of my own. And not for it to be an only child."

His answering smile had a crooked tilt. "I think it's a bit soon to start on the next one yet. Have this one first."

She laughed as joy filled her heart. "I promise you this, my darling. You won't miss out on anything."

It wasn't desire burning in his eyes, she thought. It was love. Fierce hungry love.

"Hold me, Rafe," she invited softly.

He held her. He kissed her. And Tanya knew she really had come home... blissfully safe and secure in the understanding they had at last forged together.

HARRY GRAHAM DECIDED he was probably being quixotic, but what the hell! He wanted to see Rafe and Tanya together again. When Rafe had telephoned yesterday to explain her absence from work, he had said it was okay to visit Tanya. Even said she would want to see him. So there couldn't be any problems about it. Although Rafe might have only been feeling expansive from hearing he was to be a first-time father. If so, Harry figured that wouldn't rub off in a hurry.

He checked the room numbers as he strode along the hospital corridor, found the right one, then hesitated in the doorway, feeling like an intruder on the two people who were smiling so happily at each other. He felt a sharp stab of envy and quickly stifled it. He was glad there was a different ending for them. Divorce was hell.

"I hear congratulations are in order," he said dryly, by way of announcing his arrival.

Tanya swiveled in the bed. There were bruises on her arms from her tumble down the stairs, but the expression of delight on her beautiful vivid face made nonsense of any injuries. "Harry!" she cried. "How nice of you to visit."

Rafe Carlton shot to his feet and quickly rounded the bed, his hand outstretched in greeting, a friendly grin on his face. "Good of you to be so understanding about Tanya wanting to resign," he said warmly. "She wasn't on the job very long, Harry."

Not "Graham" anymore, Harry noted in silent approval. Jealousy gone. He took Rafe's hand and returned the hearty clasp. "No worries," he assured both of them. He had always figured it would only be a temporary situation. Rafe Carlton was not the kind of man who gave up on anything he wanted. From his present manner, Harry concluded that Rafe Carlton was also very quick to learn from his mistakes.

Harry spread a grin around. "I always thought babies would be more important to Tanya than working for me." *If only Helen had wanted one... but no point in thinking about that now.*

"Well, she's going to be helping me out in my business, too, aren't you, darling?" Rafe said.

Tanya glowed with pleasure. "As much as I can."

"Your wife is a tiger for detail, Rafe. One of the best," Harry declared approvingly, then moved over to the bed and presented Tanya with the posy he had bought for her. "The blue cornflowers are for a boy. The pink carnations are for a girl. I'm covering all bets."

She laughed and glowed up at him. "Thank you, Harry. And thank you for everything else too. You're a very nice man, and a very wise one."

He waggled his eyebrows consideringly. "Okay. I'll accept that." He turned a wry expression to Rafe. "Though maybe I'd do better if I were a sexy man."

"Not necessarily," Rafe retorted with a wry twist back. "That can have its problems, too."

Harry managed a laugh. "Okay. I'll accept that," he said good-humoredly, covering the hurt that still pulsed from Helen's choice of a brainless hunk.

"When Tanya feels up to it, you must come and have dinner with us one night, Harry," Rafe invited.

"Yes, do say you will," Tanya pressed eagerly.

"Love to," Harry said. And meant it. There was so much damned misery in the world, it was a rare pleasure to be in the company of a couple who shone with happiness. Not only that, this was clearly an offer of friendship and one he would like to explore. Even if nothing eventuated from it, he would at least have one less lonely night.

DAVID JAMES CARLTON was christened on a fine Sunday morning ten months later. After the church service, Tanya and Rafe hosted a family party at their home. It was a particularly joyous occasion. As Rafe showed off his infant son to everyone, and Tanya looked on indulgently, she felt she couldn't possibly be happier.

"He is the image of you, Rafe," Sophia clucked, looking adoringly at her new grandson.

"No, he's not, Mamma," Rafe protested. He hitched the baby higher in the crook of his arm and pointed out the one feature that belied his mother's boast. "He has Tanya's dimple. See?" His finger pressed softly on the tiny indentation that centered his son's chin. The look of adoration on Rafe's face outshone Sophia's.

Tanya could not help smiling to herself. Rafe, the proud father. He was reveling in this christening party with all his family gathered together to pay homage to *his* child.

It seemed so hugely ironic that she had once thought a baby might be a divisive wedge in their marriage. They had never been closer together than they were now. The special intimacy of sharing the birth of their child, sharing the joy of his tiny perfection, sharing every new experience with him.

Life was beautiful.

She noticed Harry hoisting Rafe's nephew onto his shoulder, the little boy giggling delightedly at his new stepfather. Tanya shook her head bemusedly. Who would have thought that Harry and Rafe's widowed sister would get together? Yet quite clearly they had been smitten with each other from their first meeting. Tanya remembered it well. Neither she nor Rafe had thought of any matchmaking. They had simply invited Theresa to balance the table when they had asked Harry to dinner. Tanya was enormously pleased for both of them.

The voice of Bea Wakefield intruded on her whimsical thoughts. "Do you think, if I asked Rafe nicely, he would let me hold my great-grandchild for a little while?"

Tanya laughingly turned to the indomitable lady at her side. "Of course, Grandma."

The hazel eyes twinkled at Tanya. "There is one thing I want to tell you before I deprive Rafe of his son."

"Yes, Grandma?"

"It's about your grandfather."

"What?" Tanya could hardly remember him. He had died when she was five years old. He was a vague shadowy figure who used to give her horse rides on his knee.

Her grandmother's eyes softened wistfully. "Oh, nothing really. But you remember when you ran away from Rafe?"

"Yes, Grandma."

"That was wicked of you, Tanya," Bea chided.

"Yes, Grandma." Suitably chastened.

"And there were certain things you thought you couldn't tell me."

Tanya did some inner squirming. "Yes, Grandma."

"You shouldn't have been ashamed." Bea's lips curled into a dry little smile and there was quite a wicked twinkle in the bright hazel eyes. "I do know all about it, Tanya. Your grandfather was the very devil himself in bed."

Tanya's mouth was agape, her eyes widely staring after her grandmother, as that redoubtable figure of rectitude relieved Rafe of his son. Having been deprived of their child, Rafe made his way straight to Tanya, giving her a quizzical look as he drew her into his arms.

"Something wrong, darling?"

"No." She recovered herself and smiled up at him. "You know, Rafe, I think Grandma understands a lot more than I gave her credit for."

His responding smile was a trifle rueful. "There's a lot to be said for her simple rules."

"I didn't mean that."

Rafe drew her closer, and there was a suggestive simmer in his blue eyes that instantly quickened Tanya's pulse. "Do you think anyone would notice if we left them for about...oh...maybe twenty minutes?"

Tanya laughed, her skin instantly flushing with a rise of heat. "I think Grandma would. But I'm absolutely certain she won't say anything."

"Oh?" He cocked a wicked eyebrow at her.

"I don't think she'd mind," Tanya decided.

"Then?"

"I do feel like being ravished."

"That's one of the things I love about you, my darling," Rafe murmured in her ear as he whisked her out of the living room.

"That I like being ravished?"

"Mmm . . . you certainly do it to me. All the time, my love. From here to eternity."

my VALENTINE 1992

Celebrate the most romantic day of the year with
MY VALENTINE 1992—a sexy new collection of four
romantic stories written by our famous Temptation
authors:

GINA WILKINS
KRISTINE ROLOFSON
JOANN ROSS
VICKI LEWIS THOMPSON

My Valentine 1992—an exquisite escape into a romantic
and sensuous world.

 Harlequin Books

VAL-92-R

HARLEQUIN
PROUDLY PRESENTS
A DAZZLING NEW CONCEPT IN ROMANCE FICTION

One small town—twelve terrific love stories

Welcome to Tyler, Wisconsin—a town full of people
you'll enjoy getting to know, memorable friends and
unforgettable lovers, and a long-buried secret that
lurks beneath its serene surface....

JOIN US FOR A YEAR IN THE LIFE OF TYLER

Each book set in Tyler is a self-contained love story;
together, the twelve novels stitch the fabric of a
community.

LOSE YOUR HEART TO TYLER!

The excitement begins in March 1992, with
WHIRLWIND, by Nancy Martin. When lively, brash
Liza Baron arrives home unexpectedly, she moves
into the old family lodge, where the silent and
mysterious Cliff Forrester has been living in seclusion
for years....

WATCH FOR ALL TWELVE BOOKS OF THE TYLER SERIES
Available wherever Harlequin books are sold

Janet Dailey
Americana

A romantic tour of America through fifty favorite
Harlequin Presents novels, each one set in a different
state, and researched by Janet and her husband, Bill.
A journey of a lifetime in one cherished collection.

Don't miss the romantic stories set in these states:

Available wherever
Harlequin books are sold.

Rebels & Rogues

All men are not created equal. Some are rough around the edges. Tough-minded but tenderhearted. Incredibly sexy. The tempting fulfillment of every woman's fantasy.

When it's time to fight for what they believe in, to win that special woman, our Rebels and Rogues are heroes at heart.

Matt: A hard man to forget . . . and an even harder man not to love.

THE HOOD by *Carin Rafferty*.
Temptation #381, February 1992.

Cameron: He came on a mission from light-years away . . . then a flesh-and-blood female changed everything.

THE OUTSIDER by *Barbara Delinsky*.
Temptation #385, March 1992.

At Temptation, 1992 is the Year of Rebels and Rogues. Look for twelve exciting stories, one each month, about bold and courageous men.

Don't miss upcoming books by your favorite authors, including Candace Schuler, JoAnn Ross and Janice Kaiser.

Harlequin Regency Romance™

WHO SAYS ROMANCE IS A THING OF THE PAST?

We do! At Harlequin Regency Romance, we offer you romance the way it was always meant to be.

What could be more romantic than to follow the adventures of a duchess or duke through the glittering assembly rooms of Regency England? Or to eavesdrop on their witty conversations or romantic interludes? The music, the costumes, the ballrooms and the dance will sweep you away to a time when pleasure was a priority and privilege a prerequisite.

If you are longing for the good old days when falling in love still meant something very special, then come to Harlequin Regency Romance—romance with a touch of class.

RRG